F
EYR
1340
EYRE, KATHERINE WIGMORE
The song of a thrush

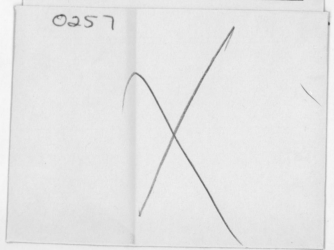

THE SONG
OF A
THRUSH

The Song of a Thrush

BY

KATHERINE WIGMORE EYRE

ILLUSTRATIONS BY

STEPHANI AND EDWARD GODWIN

New York

Henry Z. Walck, Inc.

Library of Congress Catalog Card Number: 61–14614

PRINTED IN THE UNITED STATES OF AMERICA

CONTENTS

ILLUSTRATIONS

THE SONG
OF A
THRUSH

Chapter One: A SHADOW ON THE WALL

" . . . wretches, orphans, castaways . . ."
Richard III, Act II, SCENE 2

"Poor Neddie! Was ever a worse journey? But we've no more than a scant mile ahead of us now, if yon sign post speaks true. Ludlow Town should lie round the next turn."

Peg Plantagenet, mounted on the pillion of a plodding palfrey that was splashed from fetlock to wither with rust-colored Shropshire mud, was trying her best to hearten the small, travel-weary, saddle-chafed brother who rode in front of her.

"And will we have supper soon, you think, Peg? Our uncle's castle lies close by town?"

"Close as close, thanks be to merciful Heaven. Another hour of this northern cold, and we'd be little else but ice lumps."

. Peg shivered and drew her shabby wool cloak closer under the lash of a raw December wind that had whipped back her hood and flicked a tousle of red-brown curls around her face—a small white oval of a face that might have been pretty had its mouth worn a less weary and dispirited droop.

" 'Tis set on a hill, the castle," she made herself explain

with a determined show of cheerfulness. "It rises just beyond the town walls with a river running below its ramparts.
Think on it, Neddie, fishing! All you can catch of trout
and salmon and greyling. And there be good hunting in our
uncle's preserves, so I've heard tell. Stag, for no more than
the pull of a bowstring. Fox. Badger. Hare. And a baker's
dozen when it comes to choice of land bird or waterfowl.
Oh, a splendid bailiwick indeed for a lad seeking sport! You
agree?"

"Aye—if ever we reach it. 'Twill be soon, you swear?
And what about you, Peg? Will you like it at our uncle's as
well as I?"

"Most assuredly. Why not, pray?"

Peg's answer was quick, but Neddie's innocent question
had been tipped with a barb that made her wince. "Like
it?" she asked herself. Little that mattered! Year in and
year out for almost as long as memory could recall, she and
Neddie had drifted like leaves from one doorstep to another. No one had truly wanted them. No one had ever
known exactly what to do with them. And now here they
were, being blown along toward Ludlow Castle. What other
course open but to accept its belated offer of shelter? Had
she and Neddie home of their own to stand against buffet-
ing winds? Nay. Nor ever would.

Peg sighed hopelessly as she tugged at her hood. The dismal truth had been apparent long enough for her to accept
it as forever unchangeable. First inkling had dawned with
the passing of her last-year's birthday. A twelfth birthday

announcing, as it did to every maid in turn, that she had reached ripe age of consent to a marriage contract. The time had come for her to take up life as lady of a manor, with a ring upon her finger and chatelaine keys at her waist.

But, alas, who of all the page boys, the young squires and the knights of her acquaintance had shown wish for a dowerless wife? Who of them had asked for her troth? Not one.

She had been foolish and stupid to let the hurt strike so deep. Did she not know as well as anyone else that even the lowest-born lass in the land was obliged to bring more to a new rooftree than she could offer?

A chest of homespuns. A lamb. A heifer calf, perchance. A sack of corn or dried peas, at very least, or a salting of fish. Anything at all but empty hands.

Oh, the wondrous good fortune of a maid spoken for and wedded. The gladness, the thankfulness of serving lord and master. The joy of walking a path hedged peacefully and safely with the duty of ordering his household. Flax wheel and tapestry loom, beehive and herb plot, buttery and still room and bakery—all yours to put hand to. And like honey on your tongue for sweetness, the certain knowing that you need never again be lonely. Never, from your rising-up in the morning to your going to bed at night.

A most dreary word, 'lonely.' Again Peg sighed. Desperately, she longed for someone with whom to talk. Someone in whom to confide. How else, ever, could she hope to dissolve the murky doubt, the mounting distrust stirring in her as Ludlow came closer and closer with each passing mile?

But who was there to listen?

To be sure, she had Neddie. Dear Neddie. So good. So loving.

In a guilty rush Peg gave a hard squeeze to the small fur-mittened hand lying under hers, proudly, manfully guiding their palfrey's reins.

Yet how, in name of all the saints, pluck comfort from him? Neddie was too little; there lay the difficulty. Too little to remember things past. Too little to concern himself over the future. Too little by far to help her winnow truth from falsehood out of the London gossip that was the source of all her unease, her troubled thoughts. Stale gossip that had lain in her mind for years like unsprouted seed, only to spring into ugly weedy growth now that she was old enough to water it with a fearful interest, an avid yet shrinking curiosity. Gossip that whispered a horrid murderous tale of three brothers. One of them the King himself. One of them her own dead father. The third——

"Shall I find playmates a-plenty when we reach the castle, Peg? Will a great many cousins be waiting for us? Will they be glad to see us?" Neddie had twisted in the saddle to ask more of his persistent plaintive questions. "And how many be there in all, Peg? Tell me their names so that I may count. And no skipping, mind. I can say my numbers to a hundred, don't forget."

"To a hundred?" Peg, thrusting painful reflection behind her, made her gray eyes wide. "Clever indeed of you. A scholar if ever was. But before you prove it to me, what say to drawing your scarf closer? And best put an end to that coughing else you have Susan Dow turning round to goggle and scold. What's more, to open reticule and dose you."

"Susan Dow! Would that old Pinch-Mouth might fall into a mud hole! You think I'll swallow another of her nasty syrups? Not if I were hoarse as a crow." Neddie thrust out his tongue and waggled his fingers in his ears at the serving woman who was riding ahead of them between two mounted men-at-arms.

Her sodden skirts were plastered to her lean old body. Her dour face was mottled with the cold. The end of her sharp nose was blue and in a state of drip and snuffle that had lasted all the six days of their sleety, wind-blasted journey.

"Hush, Neddie. A naughty, rude wish to tumble the poor soul into a hole. You think she fancies this rough chill jogging any more than we? 'Twould sour a holy angel. But now, back to talk of our cousins, if it please you?"

Peg began to make a list, doubling down her leather-gauntleted fingers one after another. "I give you the five girls, first—our aunt and uncle be well-blest with daughters, truly. Beth is eldest, with Cecily next, if I be not mistaken, though in truth I know but little of them beyond hearsay. Anne and Katherine follow, it strikes me, with Bridgit last, and scarce out of the cradle no more than creeping and babbling."

"Enough of babes and maids—on to the boys, Peg. They be the only ones worth counting."

"Oh, so? Well, then, Edward tops the list, named for his father as you can guess, and turned twelve this past month. Best forget him as a playmate. He'll hold himself far too grownup for you, I fear me."

"But then what shall I do, among all those maids? I shan't care for it at the castle in the very least. I shall detest it!"

"Nay, 'tis not that black an outlook. You have forgotten Dickon. Cheer up. He'll find time for you. Ten is not so ancient. Quite close to eight, in fact. You will prove best of friends, doubtless."

"Dickon?" Neddie's interest quickened.

"Yes. Young Edward's brother. 'Tis a nickname given him to mark him separate from their uncle, that other Richard, who is Duke of Gloucester."

"Uncle? Then if theirs, ours as well, I take it?"

Neddie had puzzled the matter out after a moment's thought. "What a great many people to set straight in mind. We be well stocked with family, wouldn't you say, Peg?"

"True." Peg gave a brief nod. "Of a sort, that is," she amended silently. "And who would choose to claim them? Not I—not I—"

Hurriedly then, she changed the subject. "Look, a spire ahead. Only a tiny bit farther now, Neddie!"

With a slipping and scrambling of hooves on the icy

stones of an arched bridge, the travelers' horses clattered across a swollen stream. A gate in the town wall having been swung open for them, they rode on through a market square that lay quiet and empty with the coming on of dusk.

Beyond, a belfried sandstone church called for the doffing of quilled caps by Neddie and the men-at-arms, a crossing of themselves by Peg and Susan Dow, and then a few yards further on they drew rein in a cobbled stableyard.

A banging wind-twisted sign hanging from an iron bracket proclaimed the Feathers' Inn, and when a leather-aproned hostler ran out to catch at bridles and to urge a good hot supper and a Christmas Eve posset, the two men-at-arms promptly dismounted. Neddie would have slid out of his saddle with equal enthusiasm if Susan Dow had not checked him.

"No you don't, young master! Sit tight there. Tardy enough we be without further dawdling. I'll grant that pair of tipplers one small mug and not a drop more. You'll not catch me waiting about half-froze while they guzzle and swill."

She sat on her palfrey, snuffling and grumbling until her patience gave out, and then, climbing down and clucking orders for Peg and Neddie to stay where they were, she picked a way across the muddy stableyard like a wet ruffled hen, her skirts high on skinny, saffron-stockinged legs.

Teeth chattering, bones aching, Peg and Neddie obeyed her, huddling in their cloaks, their palfrey's head down against the merciless wind that was blowing little swirls of manured straw across the cobbles and stinging their chapped faces and reddening their eyes.

Neddie, trying not to cry at the thought of supper and hearth so tantalizingly close, slumped against Peg, his head on her shoulder, his velvet cap askew on a shock of brown hair.

With no better way to pass a miserable wait, Peg glanced about her. The inn's stable made a little ell behind her. Its plank door was slamming in the wind, then swinging wide again. She could hear a stomping of hoofs inside, a rustle of hay, a crunching of grain, a slobbering in a water bucket.

Shifting wearily on her pillion and turning her head, Peg saw a chestnut colt standing in a box stall. Its mane was a ripple of dark silk. A small white blazon marked the exact center of its forehead.

Now she could catch words floating from the rear of the stable.

". . . well put! A surprise packet and no mistake. Was ever quieter steed to the eye? Ungirthed, that's to say. Who'd guess it for the devil's own, once a saddle be slapped on its back? None but a smarter man than most, I'll lay my purse . . ."

The wind blew the words almost out of hearing. Peg was too exhausted, too cold, too empty-stomached to wonder with more than the faintest of interest who might be speaking. A groom, likely enough, going about his evening rounds. And, 'twould seem he had a companion. Some one else was speaking up above the monotonous slam and swing of the stable door, the swish of a broom and the ring of pitchfork tines.

". . . call it a killer and have done. What truer name for it? And handy it be as any dagger for the purpose that waits, eh? But what say to a shut mouth for you and me both, my friend? Blab out of turn, and we risk forfeiting the silver that's to come our way."

"Aye, and win chance of a noose round our necks in the bargain. Fine dancers we'd make, jerking at a rope's end."

A coarse burst of laughter drifted out of the stable but Peg did not hear it. The voices meant nothing to her. As pitifully worn-out as Neddie, she was sagging in her wooden pillion, numb with cold and dull-headed with hunger. When Susan Dow marched back across the inn yard with a foolishly grinning soldier pinched by an ear on each side of her, she had to shake both brother and sister out of a heavy stupor before their journey could begin once more.

Town dropped behind as the horses climbed a steep hill. Ludlow Castle topped the crest. Its great, gaunt square keep looked down upon a wide moor that was grown over with winter-pinched bracken and goarse. A white satin banner that boasted the three rising suns, the York rose of Edward Fourth, King of England, flew from its stone battlements.

There was no one waiting to greet Peg and Neddie as they rode up to a gatehouse set round with siege guns and sentry walk, and there was no fanfare of trumpets to announce them.

The two men-at-arms beat hard and long with their pike-staves against a barred iron gate before a surly porter, slow to leave his supper and to face the cold, troubled to open it to the orphans that the King's brother, George, Duke of Clarence, had left behind him.

With the giving and accepting of a password, they rode on through an outlying walled court where a herd of red cattle and a flock of dirty-fleeced sheep grazed on its turf and on the muddied, rain-stained fodder that had been heaped for them.

Passing a cluster of granaries and stables, barracks and armories, blacksmith and arrow makers' shops, they gained an inner paved court, and crossing by drawbridge over a sedgy moat where black swans arched their long necks and hissed among the reeds, the little cavalcade drew rein at the keep.

Another gatehouse. Again a pounding of pike staves. Again a reluctant porter shuffling out to peer and question.

This time the iron gate that fronted them was dragged open to the fierce yelps and frantic leaps of a pack of mastiffs straining the length of the steel chains that ran from their spiked collars to heavy rings set deep in the keep's wall.

Peg and Neddie and Susan Dow dismounted, and the men-at-arms took their palfries' reins and rode off for the stables at a quick clip-clop.

Once inside the keep, Susan Dow demanded a tallow candle for herself and for each of her charges and then bade

Peg and Neddie follow her up a spiral stair. Reaching the top she led the way down a long dark corridor and flung open the door of an icy bedchamber.

Musty smelling rushes were spread on the stone floor. Mildewed tapestries hung on the gray damp walls. A canopied bed, a pallet spread in a curtained alcove, an oak chest and a bench were its furnishings.

"Here you be, duckies. Fetch you I was told, and fetch you I have. So now make the best of it, that's my advice."

Susan Dow unbuckled the straps of the leather traveling sack that was slung over her shoulder like an ox yoke. "How's for togging yourselves in dry clothes? But best be quick about it—there's to be meat spread in the hall before too long."

She departed abruptly, hard on the heels of her own supper in a warm, good smelling scullery, and Peg began hurriedly rummaging in the traveling sack for a change of wardrobe.

There was a worn, out-grown brown velvet doublet and tunic for Neddie. Long brown woolen hose. Leather shoes with pointed, curled-up toes. A shabby brown velvet cap garnished with a gold and topaz brooch that was worked in the device of a sprig of yellow flowering broom, the planta genista of his royal house.

For herself there was a clean linen shift, more patched than whole. A wool petticoat. A close-fitted muslin underbodice to bind her small breasts. A forest-green damask dress, a little too scant and obviously refurbished.

Neddie, encountering difficulties with the hooks of his tunic, stood impatient and shivering while Peg clasped them and pulled his stockings straight for him. When she had done, she set about making her own self tidy.

"Hurry, do!" Neddie implored it as she smoothed her wind-roughened hair with a brush from the traveling sack and stood on tiptoe to see her face in a polished steel mirror that hung over the chest. "I be near to starving." He clutched his stomach piteously. "Did ever hear such rumblings? Naught inside me since this morning's tavern breakfast, and then no more than a bite of black bread and herring."

Peg, promising to make all speed, banished him to the alcove while she changed her dress.

Drumming his heels, he stared out of the narrow arrow-slit that served as a window in the thick stone wall. Below, far, far below, he could hear the faint splash of the river Teme as it ran over its weir. The courtyard that he peered down upon with such round curious eyes, was bright now with the windy flare of torchlight. To a noisy clang of arms and a shouting of orders, a night watch was being set on the castle's grim bastions that looked out over lonely moors and dark hills to the Welsh border.

After a moment or two, he turned to his sister a trifle dubiously. "You be quite certain that we shall like it here, Peg? A faraway place truly—and black as pitch, the countryside lying around—" All at once Neddie bolted to Peg and burrowed close. " 'Tis not that I mind, if you say that we must stay here, but oh, I be so weary! I be so hungry! And tell me truly. Peg, will we never have castle of our own for a dwelling place? Never again know a sire? A lady-mother, as you say we used?"

"No, never more, little brother." Peg put her arms around Neddie. "All of that is done for—past," she told him quietly. "What use for me to falsify? But we have each other, mind you. So away with doldrums. Have you forgot that there be a Yule feast spread below? Come, let's find it. And in less than a wink, I promise that your belly shall be round and full as a barrel. Beef, Neddie! Mutton, cheeses, cakes!"

Neddie's dolorous face brightened enormously. He took Peg's hand and they walked out into the long passageway that twisted ahead in a dim flicker of candlelight. Hesitating, no more than guessing where a stair to the great hall might lie, they started off bravely enough. But all at once as they rounded a turn, Peg's hold on Neddie's cold stubby fingers tightened. With mutual instinctive holding of their breath they stopped short, drawing close together and making themselves small behind a stone pillar.

A door ahead of them had opened. A man in black velvet doublet and hose stepped into the hall. As he took his way to the stair that they too were seeking, the wavering taper light falling from iron sconces overhead threw a dark shadow on the rough stone wall, a shadow with left shoulder higher than right.

"Who be he, think you, Peg?" Neddie blurted the question with an uneasy whisper.

"How say, at first sight? And yet from look of his hump and his limp it might well be our Uncle Richard."

"An ugly man. I don't like him." Neddie shrank against Peg. "I be afraid of him!"

"Silly boy. And fie upon you in the bargain for so unkind a tongue. Is it fault of our uncle how he be made? Or any wish of his, you think, that people call him Crook-Back?"

Peg ended her rebuke with a jerk of Neddie's hand to persuade him along the passage. But as the candle flames flared and then narrowed in the draught of the long corridor, as the shadow bobbed ahead, grotesque and somehow monstrous in its misshapeness, she confessed to herself with a sinking heart, "I be afraid, too. Sore afraid. And a fine one indeed to speak of pity—I who have learned to hate you, Your Grace of Gloucester. Hate you! Hate you!"

Chapter Two: TWO BOYS AND A BIRD

"Plots have I laid . . ."
Richard III, Act I, scene i.

Having found and descended a broad stair and with Neddie close at her skirts, Peg made her way into the castle's
banquet hall. Hung with Arras and proud tattered banners,
it was panoplied all of its great length with shield and
sword, lance and battle-axe. At its far end, leaded windows
arched to the groined roof, the glow of their ruby and sapphire glass dulled to gray by the outside darkness that lay so
heavily upon the cold solitary world stretching away to
north and west.

A thick haze of wood smoke stung her eyes as she glanced
timorously and curiously around her, and her nose wrinkled
in fastidious protest against a stench of wine fumes and candle drippings, of pitch flares and of lamp wicks fed with
rancid fish oil. Against the malodorous reek of knights and
ladies and servitors dressed in warm close wool and velvet
and leather, and of the hounds that slavered and crunched
on piles of greasy bones beside a roaring hearth fire.

When a curly-locked page stepped forward and beck-
oned, Peg followed him, inwardly quaking, to the high-

25

backed, daised chairs on which her aunt and uncle were seated.

A beauty indeed, the Queen! Most truly the rose her royal husband had named her in so many ardent sonnets. Small wonder that she had not remained maid for long, nay, nor widow either, this twice-wed Elizabeth Woodville who already boasted two stalwart, half-grown sons when the King had first come a-courting.

Were ever cheeks so smooth, so pink? As for bosom and ring-laden hands, they were no more than a shade less white than the precious miniver that edged her violet velvet train. A velvet chosen to deepen her eyes. Scarcely fair, with all that, to be the possessor of blonde hair as well. With no little envy, Peg eyed the great pale yellow knot that was drawn back under her aunt's pearled coif. Even the yards of gauzy veiling falling from the silver tissue horns of her headdress could not hide it. She was a queen with a taste for the hunt and the chase. A blue-feathered merlin falcon sat on her right wrist, leather leashed. Peg could hear the little gold bells on its legs jangling in tune with the clink of her bracelets.

But now, what of the King? Was he handsome enough to play the part of fitting spouse to Elizabeth?

Yes. In fullest measure. Peg granted it as she knelt to do homage, even though it was apparent enough that an over-fondness for the pleasures of trencher and wine cup had strained the fastenings of Edward's cloth-of-gold surcoat and pouched the flesh under his blue restless eyes. What were they searching out? What did they see, Peg wondered? He was not the happiest of men, she made quick judgement.

There was no lack of civility, however, in his welcome to her and to Neddie. None but the sharpest of observers might have suspected him of dismissing them somewhat hurriedly and with a shade of relief to the attention of the brother who stood next to his chair.

Richard Plantagenet, Duke of Gloucester, Lord High Admiral of the Kingdom, and Great Warden of the West Marches, had, in his turn, no more in the way of acknowledgement for them than a cold formal word or two and a long considering stare. A stare out of eyes that, rather than the blue of the King's, the blue that Peg's father's had been, were as dark as a toad's and as unblinking.

A toad's—a squat toad's! With a fresh shiver of revulsion, Peg remembered a dozen old-wives' tales. Misbegotten, Richard had been, from his very beginning. Ill-formed from first drawing of breath. Delivered of his poor lady mother on a night when a wind like a very tempest had raged round her castle at Fotheringay. A night when black croaking ravens and dismal-voiced magpies had swarmed the castle turret tops. A night when owls had screeched their never-failing portent of evil from the bending, cracking branches that brushed the birth-chamber windows. A night when dogs had howled in their kennels——

"Peg! Peg!" Neddie was tugging at his sister's skirts as she rose from her curtsey. "You see?" he was whispering, all agog. "The shadow! 'Tis as you thought. The shadow and our uncle be the same!"

"Shh—enough!" Peg repressed Neddie with a quick shake of her head and gave him a little butt forward that he might know it was his turn to bend knee. After that, following the curly-locked page again, they took the places that had been hastily laid for them at the end of a long trestle table. Humbling places, well below the great silver salt-cellars that marked the seats of honor close to the King and Queen.

Peg's cheeks burned. Her head went high. And yet, for all her shame and her resentment, a sting of curiosity made her glance along the board. Of what stuff, her cousins? Of what metal, that horde of yellow heads, seated at their Yule feasting? Not that she cared. Nay, less than a farthing's worth. Her opinions had long since taken shape concerning them. They were naught to her. Naught. If only they would let her bide apart from them, entirely to herself, 'twould be all she asked.

In spite of her vaunted disinterest, and under the screen of downcast russet lashes, Peg stole another look along the board. Might that be the Princess Bridgit, the little maid propped high on cushions and holding a court of her own among her fond pretty sisters? 'Twould be difficult, on second thought, to hold aloof from so sweet a babe if one were to see her daily. To own a dozen like her would be none too many.

Regard her! A very pet, all swaddled in fine linen and

It was Ned's turn to bend knee.

chewing the strings of the velvet cap that tied under her fat chin. A very rogue, banging the table with a silver spoon clutched in one little fist, dabbling the other in a puddle of milk spilled from her tipped-over silver mug.

Beyond her, higher up the table, two boys as like in face as peas in a pod, were applying themselves to heaped plates. Young Edward and Dickon, Peg guessed them, and for all the three white plumes that curled from the Prince of Wales' black velvet cap, the gold strawberry leaves and the gold rose that graced the young Duke of York's headgear, they were stuffing themselves with the same gusto as Neddie. Neddie, who, bone in hand, teeth sharp as a puppy's, was tearing at a mutton chop, a glisten of grease on his chin.

Feasting and merrymaking were in full swing now. Harps and gitterns gave out their music from the gallery above the royal chairs. Acrobats, fitted into green silk suits tight as bark on a tree, leaped and tumbled. Jugglers tossed gold balls into the air. There was the foolery of belled jesters and the mouthings of masked mummers to make the King and Queen smile. There was a minstrel lad strolling round the table spouting pretty lines regarding daisies pied and the spring song of cuckoo birds.

Best of all, to Peg's thinking, was the warmth that had begun to creep through her thin chilled body and the smell of food wafting to her nose.

Grace had been said by all at table and a hundred pewter and wooden and silver trenchers were being rushed from the scullery and buttery.

Peg was offered a choice of chicken or duck or plover. A roast peacock was passed, perched on a gold platter. Its comb and topknot had been gilded, and all the glory of its blue-green iridescent plumage had been restored to it.

Humbly seated though she was, so far below the salt, Peg was free to help herself to sizzling cuts of venison and mutton, and to pink hams and juicy, red roast beef. And there was salmon. Anchovies curled up in Spanish oil. Kidney pie, deep-crusted and oozing a dark gravy. Suet puddings. Tarts. Transparent, shaking jellies. All she wished of sugary almond paste pressed into shape of flowers and birds, fish and boar and antlered stag.

To wash the food down, there was spicy mead, fermented from gorse honey. And when the feasting was done, a wassail bowl was passed. Wassail to be drunk to the drowning of old feuds, just as the Yule log had been lighted on the hearth to burn away all the wrongs, all the evil from the year that was dying.

When it came her turn to drink, Peg barely touched lip to the bowl, and with shocked eyes watched it go its rounds.

Oh, wicked farce! Oh, mockery! How dare you quaff, Uncle Edward, while Neddie and I sit at your board? How dare you quaff, Crook-Back, so base, so cruel, if hearsay be true?

Hearsay. Hearsay—to believe, or not to believe?

With a deliberate wrench, Peg looked away. To fasten her thoughts elsewhere, she asked herself who the boy might be seated between the Prince of Wales and his sister Beth. A boy older than herself. Sixteen, or thereabout. A boy with grave hazel eyes and a casque of shining smooth hair. Gold hair, brighter than the flaxen locks of the King and Queen and their brood.

Another princeling, was he? Nay. Too marked a lack of jewels or other richness about his gray wool tunic. A youth serving squireship toward the gaining of spur and sword more like it, from look of the crimson badge sewn to his sleeve.

Peg slanted another glance under her lashes.

She had made a polite curtsey to the boy earlier, on her way down a long line of courtiers to kneel before the King. The page she had followed had announced his name among a dozen others. What was it? Richard Pole?

But with so many Richards here at Ludlow Castle, how ever could one keep them separate? Yet come to think on it, Dickon had been given a little special name to set him apart, so why not one for this boy? Would Sir Golden Cap do? Yes. 'Twas perfect. It came to tongue without half trying. Golden Cap. Sir Golden Cap.

Pleased though she was with the ring of it, there was little time for Peg to mull the nickname she had coined so readily. Silver basins filled with warm, herb-scented water were being passed round the board for the dipping of greasy sticky fingers, and linen napkins held out for their wiping.

When that was done, a tall, thick candle of finest white beeswax was set in the middle of the table. The Christmas Candle. It would be kept carefully burning for days, Peg knew, set in its stone socket that was fashioned in the image of the Holy Lamb. Only when Twelfth Night came, would it be allowed to gutter. And now, with the solemn lighting of its wick, there was to be a giving of gifts up and down the table. Not a happy moment for a beggar who had nothing to offer on her own part.

Peg could only wish herself leagues away as she sat, hot-cheeked, murmuring stiff inaudible little thank-yous for every present passed down the table to her.

She didn't want them. She didn't want them. And there were a surprising number of them. Silk ribands, kerchiefs, pommander balls, a gold bodkin, a velvet hawking glove, silver shoe buckles. Beth and Cecily and Katherine and Anne had plucked them with hasty generosity from their own over-abundance.

Their cousins' arrival had been unexpected and awkward. No one had thought that Peg and Neddie would surmount wind and sleet and muddy highways in time to arrive by Christmas Eve.

Young Edward and Dickon were equally concerned and generous. A ball and a racquet found their way to Neddie from the Prince, and an ash-wood fish pole that threatened to poke out every eye at the table as it was passed along.

Dickon made a real sacrifice. He parted with a pile of lead soldiers first, and then he gave up a little silver cart with wheels that turned at the pull of a string.

Even His Grace, the Duke of Gloucester, entered into the gift giving. Emptying a silk purse that hung at his belt, he sent gold pieces spinning in every direction. Two of them were tossed toward Peg and Neddie with a careless "Catch, niece! Catch, you there, nephew."

Neddie grabbed his coin delightedly, but Peg, feigning to miss the toss, let hers tinkle to the floor. Had there been a darkening of His Grace's face and a curl to his lips as he shrugged and turned away, or had she but imagined it?

A noisy shoving back of benches put end to Peg's private queries. Her royal cousins had jumped up from the table clamoring for a round of games, and a horde of their friends from among the castle's less highborn children were swarming into the hall from scullery and stable, shepherd's hut and weaver's cot.

Yule Eve! Yule Eve! Let no one miss the fun. Whether she would or not, Peg was caught up in the wild merriment.

When it came to a question of what to play first, Hot Cockles proved a general favorite. The sport was rough and ready. Shouts of glee greeted each selection of a victim, whoever it might be. In due course by the drawing of straws, it was Peg's turn to kneel down in the middle of the hall, blindfolded, her hands behind her back. One by one the others ran past her shrieking with laughter, prince and princess as rowdy as peasant or milkmaid.

Thwack! Thwack! Guess who pummels you! Guess who! Guess who! Name your tormentor or stay upon your knees until you do!

Because Peg was a stranger and knew so few names to call out, she took more than a fair share of blows. One thump in particular, accompanied by a hard poke, toppled her off balance and sent her sprawling on the floor—a rough floor, for all its strewing of rushes and its scattering here and there of rare Turkey rugs.

There was a further burst of laughter and the pouncing upon of another scapegoat as she tried to gain her feet.

"Be you hurt, Mistress Margaret?"

The boy whom Peg had dubbed Sir Golden Cap was offering her a steady hand and helping her to untie the knots of her blindfold.

"Not too badly, I thank you, Master Pole. A scrape, a bruise or two—" Peg rubbed an elbow, and touched a knee gingerly with a rueful "Oooh! Methinks I've lost a bit of skin."

"It smarts, does it? Best try a smear of salve. Sorrel, or——"

Sir Golden Cap had no chance to prescribe further. With the on-rush of another wild game, he and Peg were swept apart.

It was hide-and-seek now. There was a scramble for partners, and in the merry confusion, no less a personage than Young Edward himself, snatched at Peg's sleeve. "Off we go, coz! I know where to duck." He dragged Peg after him and gave her a quick shove behind a fall of heavy tapestries that hung against a far wall. "What say to this? 'Tis snug and secret here as in a badger's hole to my way of thinking. They'll search all the night through before they find us."

There had been little use of Peg protesting, none at all in

pulling against Young Edward's determined hold on her wrist. Before she knew it, crowded next to him in the hot smothering pocket he had chosen, Peg was discovering to her surprise that the game of hide-and-seek had a certain zest to it. She actually found herself clapping hand to mouth to stifle an excited giggle as seeker after seeker dashed unsuspectingly past.

And refuse though she would to admit to herself that it might be possible to enjoy even so much as a single moment in company with any member of the royal family, she nevertheless began to take stock of Young Edward with the same sidelong glances and the same lively curiosity that she had given way to at the banquet table.

A quite ordinary everyday boy, that was plain to see. Prince of Wales or not, he had a dirty face, dust-streaked from the folds of the tapestry that closed them in with its nose-tickling, sneeze-provoking smell of wool and linen and tarnished gold thread. One would judge him scarce older than Neddie to hear him chatter on concerning this or that, and more especially the gifts that Yule Eve had brought him. A youth with tongue hung in the middle! How he was crowing over those Christmas prizes. How sparkling his blue blue eyes, even in the darkness of what he chose to call a badger's hole.

One gift, in particular, would seem to have brimmed his cup of delight to overflowing. A colt.

Young Edward's face was glowing. Had his Cousin Peg heard tell of it, he wanted to know, eagerly, proudly? Nay?

Then she had missed something, indeed! He would enlighten her without further delay.

The colt of which he spoke was a chestnut, an Arab of purest stud. Oh, a prize if ever was! No one, no one at all in the kingdom, nor even across far seas, could boast finer mount. And it would be his, his alone, in a few short hours.

And where was it at the moment?

Bedded down in a stall in Ludlow Town, Young Edward explained to Peg. The colt had been brought all the way from his Uncle Richard's stables in London. Its journey had been severe. Its arrival delayed by storms, washed-out roads. And now, a rub for its sleek flanks and a serving of hot mash had seemed the wiser course, rather than further excursion on so cold a night. But on the morrow—the glorious morrow!

"The colt is a chestnut, you say, Your Highness?"

As she asked the question, Peg was remembering vaguely the inn yard where she had waited that afternoon, and the swing and slam of a stable door. But to think, even briefly, about the sleety bitter wind that had tormented her and the galling pillion she had sat upon set her to shivering and aching again.

How long the day had been! How wearisome!

Peg swallowed a yawn and yearned all at once for bed. Then mindful of her manners, she asked politely and with what little wide awakeness and interest she could muster, "Your steed has a name, Your Highness?"

"Yes. Or will have, rather, on the morrow when I mount

him. 'Gweno' strikes me as a sound choice. None better, considering. 'Tis a Welsh name meaning 'star.' "

" 'Star?' But why?"

The aptness of the colt's name remained undisclosed.

A sudden clamor of bells rang out, and Young Edward thrust aside the tapestries. "Quickly, coz! Games be done. 'Tis the stroke of midnight. Time now for Mass."

Once out of the badger's hole, Peg saw that a reverent sobering had fallen upon the Great Hall. A chamberlain running to Young Edward proffered a towel and ewer so that he might wash his face. Dickon had been commanded to sit on a bench and catch his breath and cool his blazing cheeks after a riotous game of tag. Princess Beth had drawn a little prayer missal from her bodice. Princess Anne had been given a pin to catch up a loosened silk garter. Princess Bridgit's under-swaddling had been hastily changed for dry linen, and a milky pap-rag had been thrust in her mouth for the comforting of her sleepy wailing.

Everyone in the hall fell into a quiet line.

With their King and Queen leading the way, all the Yule revelers filed out into the courtyard.

A company of monks and a purple-robed bishop waited them at the door of the royal chapel, their frozen breath ascending like incense on the still air. Wind and sleet were over. A few stars had struggled through the breaking clouds.

Once inside the round stone nave everyone knelt down. Because the walls were hung with bay and holly and fir,

Peg felt as though she were embraced by the arms of a sweet-smelling forest.

A song went up from all who had gathered together.

> *Veni, Jesu, Redemptor omium!*
> *Veni—*
> *Veni—*

Would the Christ Child hear it, Peg wondered? Would He answer by coming down to earth to be born again as He had on so many other Yules? Surely one should beg it of Him with all one's heart.

She sang a little louder. And with her clear piping, some of the fear and some of the doubt that had plagued her for so long began to lessen inside her. What, after all, could London's horrid gossip have been but ugly lies?

Edward the King was kneeling at the altar rail this very moment. Crook-Back was kneeling, too. Would either of them dare be there, supplicating God, if they were truly as wicked as she had so foolishly allowed herself to believe?

Nay. Never!

An hour later when the chapel bells were silent, and when Neddie was already asleep on his pallet and Peg was undressing, Susan Dow shuffled unceremoniously into their bedchamber.

A thin gray rat-tail braid hung out from under her muslin nightcap. A soiled, puce-colored wrapper dragged at her heels. She was carrying a candle and a little cage fashioned of plaited reeds.

There was a bird in the cage, a silent moping thrush.

"For you, my pretty." Susan Dow banged the cage down on the oak chest. "Take it and welcome."

Peg unhooking her bodice paused to stare. "For me?"

" 'Tis what I said. Be you deaf? And sent you from His Highness, the Prince."

"The Prince? You mean Young Edward sends it? But why? Whatever for? And what ails the poor bird? A most mournful look to it, so huddled and still."

"Small wonder. 'Twas picked up on the moor, froze stiff and with a wing broke."

"His Highness found it?"

"Aye, a day ago."

"But I don't understand—why send the thrush to me?"

" 'Twas your warbling in chapel this eve that did it. Lawks, mistress, a birdie yourself!" Susan Dow interrupted her explanation to scratch vigorously. She picked something alive out of the folds of her wrapper, scrutinized it with interest, whatever it might have been, and then disposed of it with a snap of her fingernails. "More than one heard you," she went on, "and when His Highness cocked an ear, he took a zany notion that mayhap you'd find a way to perk up Droop-Head here. Naught would do but that I climb the stairs on the instant and hand over the bird without a min- ute's wait. Stuff and nonsense to the whole matter, I say. Master Thrush will be dead as dead by sun-up. Wring his neck and have done; why not? Pop him in a pie, that's my view!" With a cackle and a snuffle, Susan Dow took herself off to bed.

Peg opened the cage door. The thrush fluttered wildly as her hand closed over it, and its heart was a hard throb in its white-feathered breast.

"I shan't hurt you." Peg spoke to it gently as she examined a dragging wing. "Perchance I can make you well again. Tell me, did His Highness not know enough to bind your break? Fie on him, his thoughts are on naught but the coming of that colt of his, I'll wager. No matter. 'Tis not too late for succor. There be time a-plenty to heal you. And once you feel more blithe we shall have the singing lessons that the Prince asks of us. But 'twill be you who is music master when it comes to the teaching of hedgerow songs. Oh yes, little bird, for you know far more than I of hawthorn bloom and of wild plum blowing."

She wadded one of her wool stockings into a nest in a corner of the cage and set the thrush upon it. After she had covered the cage with a padded wool petticoat, she blew out her candle and climbed into bed.

The linen sheets were clammy against her stiff aching body. It was difficult to get to sleep. Peg shivered wretchedly. Her teeth chattered. Then at long last the heaped feather quilts and the drawn bed curtains began to cup a delicious soothing warmth.

Drowsily Peg considered the morrow. A pleasanter prospect now than she had imagined possible. First off, she would clean the thrush's cage. Disgraceful, its neglected state. Young Edward was in need of a stern taking to task. Next she would splint the little bird's broken wing. A labor not too difficult to attempt if she went about it with care, and granted that the thrush did not die of fright. And then when its fears calmed, as she trusted they would, she would do her best to coax a chirp from it. Was Young Edward right? On hearing her sing, might the thrush find heart for trill of its own again?

Young Edward.

A boy who could listen if he chose to the music of a hundred lutes. A boy who could command a score of minstrels to sing for him. And yet a boy who cared about a moor bird's song.

And Sir Golden Cap, he of the shining hair, who had helped her up from the floor, was another kindly youth. And of most pleasing countenance as well. Her bruised elbow and her scraped knees did not pain her near so sharp remembering him.

Chapter Three: STABLE AND HALTER

"What stay had we but Clarence? and he's gone."
Richard III, Act II, scene 2.

Peg woke to a chanticleer chorus. Drowsily she sat up in bed to listen to the courtyard cocks crowing lustily, as ever on Christmas morning, that onslaught of witch or devil might be fended off from so holy a day.

Darkness was departing, but a last pale sentinel star gleamed through the window slit of her stone chamber. As Peg snuggled back under the covers, her thoughts drifted to another star—to Gweno, the colt of which Young Edward had boasted so proudly.

The most beautiful colt in all the world. Incomparable. Beyond price.

Peg's red mouth curved in a little sleepy smile. An eager boy, surely, Young Edward. Was ever gift more impatiently waited than this steed of his? 'Twas plain to any eyes that he longed for it as he had never longed for anything in his princely life before. His heart's one desire—to swing leg over saddle, to put hand to rein——

How great her cousin's envy, if he knew that she had

already caught glimpse of that glorious steed of his. For now, lying cozily under the heaped quilts, cold and hunger forgot and travel weariness abated, her dull heavy head clearing and in far less of a muddle than it had been the night before, she was beginning to think that Young Edward's promised mount was the very colt that she had seen in the stable of the Feathers' Inn. The chestnut with the white blazon on its forehead. A blazon that could so readily be described as a star.

But what was it that she had overheard concerning the colt? A tag end of talk had floated out from the stable she remembered vaguely. Talk that defamed Young Edward's Christmas colt rather than praised it.

Peg groped deep through hazy recollection, and then she started up in bed again, roused all at once into far fuller wakefulness than she had been by cock crow. Two words came to mind—"killer" and "dagger." But who had voiced them? Stable grooms, yes, but were they the same grooms, wearing Richard of Gloucester's livery, who had fetched the colt from London?

And if they were, what meaning in those two words of theirs? Had their loose conniving tongues given way a dreadful plot? Had they unwittingly laid bare to the bone the truth of their master's wickedness?

Two and two made four, ever. And here were pieces of a puzzle clicking into shape. Gweno, a Yule gift from a kind and generous uncle to a beloved nephew. Gweno, so beautiful to look upon. But a Gweno declared to be the devil's own under saddle. Oh, anyone, anyone at all, could picture what was going to happen.

Only let Young Edward swing onto the colt's back, girthstraps buckled tight for his first ride; only let him press boot heel to flank, and he would be flung to the ground. And there he would lie, dead, if Richard of Gloucester's secret wish came true. Dead of a twisted neck or broken skull that could not be mended.

Dead. A blue-eyed boy who someday was meant to sit a throne.

She saw it all.

Shaken, sick, Peg cowered in her bed. All of her old fears, her doubts and her repulsion against His Grace of Gloucester were rushing back upon her like a swirling torrent of mill water that had burst its dam. No use now to try to stem the flood again, as she had done the night before on her knees in a bough-sweet chapel.

The truth was out. At long last it lay in the open. All that had been obscure to her in the past had been made clear. All that lay ahead was in plain sight. Crook-Back would do away with Young Edward as ruthlessly as he had murdered her father.

To be sure, it had been the King himself who had sent her father to the Tower on a charge of treason. The King who had set signature to his death warrant. The King who had shorn herself and Neddie of their royal rank, their rights of inheritance. Attainted them, as it was called by law.

But she knew now that it was Richard who had been at
the bottom of it all, just as London had gossiped, just as ru-
mor had hinted to her. Deftly, with cleverest guile, Crook-
Back had set brother against brother. Fermented disagree-
ment between them. Stirred jealousies. Carried lies on his
lips to both of them.

Oh, loathsome Richard. A toad, verily. A slug. A thing
dredged up from slime——

And cruel, cruel Edward. Yes, cruel as Crook-Back, every
bit, and to be as greatly hated.

And yet—and yet—thinking on him——

Wondering, wondering, Peg tried to shape an honest pattern out of the scraps of her half-knowledge and the welter
of her bewildering ignorance.

In fairness, what measure of blame for her father's death
lay at Edward's door? Had his hand been forced? The
Crown, first and always. If you were born to the purple
you were taught that with your earliest breath. And down
with traitors! Down with usurpers! You learned to cry that
too, for how else hold your kingdom together?

Reluctantly, Peg granted two sides to a question that
had worn but one for her until that moment.

Had her father been greedy? Had he been guilty, no
matter who craftily urged him on, of reaching out for a
scepter that did not belong to him? Had he crashed his
world down around him with his own hands? How would
she ever know? All that she could remember of him lay in

the locket round her neck. The little seed-pearl locket with his painted likeness inside. The locket held her mother's face as well. Dead Isabelle Neville, who had been daughter to that earl once called the King-Maker. The King-Maker. Peg considered the name soberly. Her grandfather.

What was it that made people long so to lay hands upon a crown? She wished that someone could please explain it. For herself, she saw no slightest worth to one. A crown but hurt your head. Weighted you down. Even now, her Uncle Edward's gold circlet rested over-heavily, people whispered.

Whispers. Whispers. Did no one ever speak out? She wished one would! And was it true, that wretched tale going the rounds of London of the King washing his hands more oft than needed these days as though to rid them of a red stain that he alone saw? Was it true that he was trying his best to drown his conscience, and a ghost, in the dregs of his wine cup?

The faintest possible pity stirred in Peg. What, after all, was King Edward, but a sorry dupe? And now, if Gweno the Star, and Gweno the Killer, proved to be indeed one and the same, another weight would press upon him. He would learn what it was to weep, and so would his yellow-haired Queen and pretty Beth and Cecily and Katherine and Anne and Dickon.

But why give thought or concern to her royal relatives? Her liking for them had been little enough when she first arrived at Ludlow Castle. Let Richard of Gloucester have his way. She had only to keep a shut mouth and a chance would be hers to even a dozen old scores. By no more than nipping back the soft foolish pity so newly springing in her for her Uncle Edward, she could lay hand upon a naked sword. It was hers for the drawing. Blow for blow she could strike back at the King a hundredfold. That, for her father's murder! Call him usurper or not, she had loved him! Loved him! Loved him!

The sting of hot rebellious tears made Peg reach for the hem of her linen sheet that she might wipe them away before they slid down her cheeks to the pillow.

That, too, for her snatched-away home! For the castle in Warwickshire set among beeches and oaks. For the river Avon, flowing so quietly through its grassy park.

And that, and that, for Neddie! The shameful word 'attainted' meant that he had lost the right to strive for knighthood. Their Uncle Edward knew full well that a boy, growing up stripped of spurs and pride, had lost even more than a maid robbed of her dowry. Had that knowledge stayed his hand? Not for an instant.

The morning star faded as Peg lay hugging old hurts close. Gray light began to filter through the arrow-slit. Savory smelling smoke blew up from the scullery. There was a rattle of pitchers and buckets, the creak of a winch at the courtyard well. A tramp of feet, a shouted command as the night watch changed along the castle ramparts. And with the beginning of a new day, the chapel bells rang out their Christmas matins.

Dong! Dong!
Venite, venite, exultemus!
Laudate Dominum!
Dong! Dong! Dong!

There was no shutting out their sweet clangor. Peg suddenly had tossed back the quilts and was springing out of bed.

Shame upon her! Was the dawn of Christ's birthday a morning for the harboring of grudges? Nay. Nay. Alack, that cock crow had been in vain. All too many witches and devils were yet about, eager to tempt an unwary soul into every sort of evil thinking, evil doing. A narrow escape, truly, from mortal sinning.

Peg crossed herself thankfully, hurriedly. And now, kind heaven, let her be in time—let her be in time! Or had she already dallied too long in bed?

It was she alone who could keep Young Edward off his colt. She alone who could manage it, she knew, as she struggled with cold awkward fingers to lace her bodice and hook her skirt, the while she turned one wild hasty plan and then another over in her mind.

No one, not a person in the castle, would listen twice to her tale of Gweno the Killer. She would be scoffed at, and then, doubtless, she would be locked away in some dark hole and whipped for a lie-monger, a mischief-maker—though the whipping would be naught to her, so long as her black dungeon held no rats.

With a shiver that had little to do with the cold, Peg

hugged her cloak around her, pulled up its hood, and as quietly as possible, that Neddie would not waken, she drew back the door bolt and slipped into the dark silent passageway. Scurrying to the porter's stair, she crept down unseen and let herself into the courtyard.

No one stopped her. No one paid slightest heed to her in the bustle of early morning routine; and it was not yet light enough for a bold stare or a whistle from soldier or groom or kennel man who otherwise might have been interested in a comely face and a pair of well-turned ankles.

Luck was still with her at the outer wall. A train of ox carts had begun to rumble through the gate, bound for town with a load of royal Christmas gifts for the abbot of St. Lawrence's church to distribute among his poor. Sacks of grain. Barrels of ale. Bales of warm, woolen cloth. Beef and mutton. Faggots cut from the King's forests. Medicines brewed in the Queen's still room.

Not knowing in the least where she found the courage, Peg pushed a way through a crowd of porters and teamsters and climbed into the rear of the last cart. In her shabby cloak and her worn shoes, and without gloves on her cold-reddened hands, she might have been a servant maid, a woodcutter's daughter, bent on a holiday jaunt and more than a little glad to ride rather than plod into town.

The rutted muddy road unwound down the hill, and then when the carts drew up in front of St. Lawrence's, Peg found it quite simple to climb down in the confusion of unloading, and dart away.

To the best of her memory, the Feathers' Inn lay no more than a pebble toss from the church. Over there it should be, to her left hand. When she came on its painted wooden sign, she dared to open a gate the merest crack, sidle through, and hugging a wall, creep to the stable. A small ragged hostler boy was sprawled across the threshold fast asleep, a horse blanket rolled under his head for a pillow. He was no older than Neddie, Peg saw, as she stepped back, only barely in time to keep from stumbling over him. A pale, hungry-looking little urchin. Had His Grace of Gloucester's grooms persuaded him with kicks and cuffs and perchance promise of a ha'penny to stand watch over Gweno while they cele-brated Yule Eve? Little other reason for his being there.

The boy slept without stirring, while Peg edged past him and tiptoed to the box stall where the chestnut colt stood. The moment she came close, its head went up, and it whinnied a welcome.

"Quiet, quiet, Gweno, please!"

With her heart pounding, Peg laid a hand on the colt's neck. The flow of its silk mane was warm and rippled. Its flanks bore the burnish of bright armor.

Would the colt rear? Strike at her? Peg answered herself quickly, trying not to be afraid. Nay. There was no slight-est danger. It was only the cinching of a girth strap that would goad Gweno to deviltry. All she had any intention of doing was to fasten a halter around his neck. The halter that hung there just above him on the stall wall.

Her plans were made, and yet as she patted Gweno, and

as he quieted under her pleading and even muzzled in her neck, Peg was close to abandoning them.

Surely, surely, imagination had run away with her? Yesterday's weariness had played a trick upon her? If she had heard them speaking at all, must not those loose-tongued grooms have had some other colt in mind? Not Gweno, not Young Edward's Star. For how could this soft-eyed nuzzling creature become a changeling that would do him to death?

She had let imagination run away with her. She was playing the part of a simpleton, a silly meddling fool. The sooner she took herself back to the castle the better.

Wavering, pulled this way, pulled that, Peg hesitated. Her eyes went to the stable door. How easy to slip out. How much wiser—safer.

The hostler boy stirred a little. Quickly, before she could change her mind again, and while there was yet time left her, Peg reached for the colt's halter and buckled it round his neck. He stood quiet, his velvet nose poking inquisitively at her hood until he had pushed it back and brought her hair tumbling around her face.

With a soft scolding and another pat of his neck, she led him out of the stall. When a mouse rustled in the hay, she stopped short. With the creak of a door swinging somewhere on a loose hinge, cold drops trickled along her spine. She would have let go the halter and run, had she known which way to bolt, which way safety lay.

There was nothing to do but wait until the stable was quiet again and unmenacing. After that she made herself veer past the little sleep-sodden boy sprawled on the stable threshold, with no more than a margin of inches between his small body and the brush of her skirts, the light high-stepping of the colt.

Next came the inn yard to cross, mired in slushy ice and mud. Then the gate to open. Now there was town to leave behind and the wide empty moor to gain. As she hurried along the unfamiliar twisting streets, the clatter of the colt's hooves on the cobbles was terrifyingly loud in her ears.

The whole town would hear!

Her fears proved groundless. Even though a dog or two set up a barking, not a single villager popped a night-capped head out of a door. A late deep sleep for everyone, that was the way of it on Christmas morning, thanks to the jolly handing-round of punch bowls, the lifting of mugs, the night before.

Peg reached the edge of the moor unchallenged.

She stood for a moment looking about uncertainly. There was a soughing of wings over her head as a flight of wild swan cut the gray sky. The early sun had set a pewter luster to it. Each frost-rimed twig of gorse that caught at her skirt, each silvered winter-brittle thorn bush glittered like glass. The feet of a startled scuttling hare made a hollow drumming on ground that was iron-hard with cold.

When her anxious hurried seeking lit upon a copse of dark huddling trees that offered shelter for the colt, Peg slipped off his halter. He stood for a moment snuffing and then, with a neigh like a trumpet call, he was away, cantering first, and then breaking into a swift gloriously free gallop.

Peg watched him until he was out of sight. No one now would ever catch him. No one, ever again, would saddle him. He would learn to paw the moor's frosty crust and to graze on the turf that lay under it. He would find a glen, running with water to drink. And in the spring, he would take a mate from among the wild shaggy Welsh ponies that roamed the moor.

He would always be Gweno. Always the Star, never the Killer.

Chapter Four: A WAGER

"Have not to do with him, beware of him—"
Richard III, Act I, SCENE 3.

Turning her back upon the moor Peg began an uphill trudge to the castle. A yawning stretching porter passed her through the gatehouse and again, thanks to the courtyard's early bustle, no one bothered to question her coming or going.

Neddie was still asleep when she peeked behind the alcove's crimson curtain. He was clutching a lead soldier in each fist. The little silver cart with wheels that turned lay close beside him on the pillow.

Peg shook him. "Wake up! Wake up, sleepy head! Milk and oatmeal wait you."

Neddie opened his eyes to stare and blink and then screwing them shut he burrowed deeper into the bedclothes. Peg shook him again and tugged at the quilts. The cold struck him and he sat up shivering, to protest and to berate her. Then his eyes lighted on the silver cart. Letting go his soldiers he snatched it up with such fierce delight that Peg had to pry it loose from his fingers and threaten him direly before he would set about the pulling on of his curling-toed slippers and the splashing of his face in the basin of icy water she poured for him from a pewter ewer.

When they went down to the Great Hall they found that their cousins were already at breakfast. Young Edward, having cleaned his plate as though a race were on, was urging Richard Pole to put down knife and spoon. "—a second helping? Now I know you for a glutton as well as a tortoise. Faster there. Faster! How oft must I remind you that my colt waits to be fetched from town? And have you forgot your promise to watch me mount?"

"Not for a moment, Your Highness, but first you'll grant me leave to stow a little something under my belt? The inner man wants satisfying." Richard Pole helped himself to bread and sausage and porridge. "Why the hurry, can you tell me? Be this wondrous Gweno of yours the first and only steed you ever straddled? One would think it! Let him cool his heels, I say, till you've downed a bite of that meat pie, yonder. And as I confess a fondness for beef-and-kidney myself, might it be passed along?"

"A foolish waste of time, eating!" Young Edward shoved back his plate. "Come along. See with your own eyes what an Arab colt be like. And let me tell you, my friend, you'll find that Gweno makes naught but clumsy plough-plodders out of all other nags in the castle stables."

His eyes were jubilant, confident. As he hooked an arm through Richard Pole's and swaggered eagerly out of the Hall, Peg found her breakfast dry in her mouth, sticking in her throat. Difficult, too, the making of conversation with

Young Edward's sisters who gathered close to the hearth, when they had finished at table, to toast their velvet-slippered toes while they matched bright skeins of tapestry wools or busied themselves at their looms.

Making her curtseys as soon as she dared, she wandered aimlessly back to her cold bedchamber. It was only then that she remembered the broken-winged songless bird that Susan Dow had left in her care. She had even forgotten to show it to Neddie, and the reed cage, covered as it was with her petticoat, had escaped his notice.

Remorsefully, she hurried to make up for her neglect. Scooping the thrush into her hand, she examined it carefully, and managed, for all its wild fluttering, to bind its dragging wing close to its body with a length of linen thread from her sewing box.

She cleaned the cage then and filled its little water dish and went down the backstairs to the scullery to beg a scrap of suet and a cupful of meal. All the while that the thrush huddled in its feathers, its heart beating so hard that it might well have burst its breast, Peg knew a dreadful fear of her own. What would happen when Young Edward found Gweno gone? What would happen? What would happen?

Somehow the morning dragged by and then at noontime, with the jangle of refectory bells, Neddie rushed in on her, his round eyes big, his cheeks bright banners of excitement. "Peg. Peg. Guess what!"

He ignored the thrush in its cage. All that mattered was the heralding of his courtyard news. "There's to be a flogging. A flogging of a stable boy. 'Tis declared so by our Uncle Richard. And in the barrack-yard, for everyone to watch. Not today, it being Holy Christmas, nor tomorrow, with further feasting to be done, but on the day following, in mid-morning. A flogging, I say, Peg! Be you listening? And you should see the rage our cousin the Prince stews in. He be boiling!"

"And the cause of his anger?" Peg's stiff lips barely framed the question.

"It be the loss of his colt that has raised the hubbub. That promised Yule gift of which he was boasting at breakfast, you remember, Peg? But when he went down to the town to fetch it he found it gone. Clean gone."

Neddie was savoring every detail of his news. "Stolen from the inn stable, mind you! Led away by a thief, its halter off the wall, the stable door swinging wide. Did ever hear the like? And glad I am not to be the hostler's boy who slept through it all, I can tell you."

Neddie's eyes were rounder than ever. "The flogging is only half. More than that, he's to be strung up by his thumbs. A lesson for the whole of the castle to mark, our uncle calls it. And if we wish a close stand to see it, Peg, we shall have to be out of our beds early that morn—there'll be a crowd and no mistake."

"A crowd? And you think I'd join them to crane at so horrid a sight?" Peg stared at Neddie aghast. "Nay, nor shall you. You shan't. You shan't. I won't let you."

"Shan't? Won't?" It was Neddie's turn to stare. "You'd

dare set such words against our uncle's command? We have to be there. Everyone does! And why fly in such a tizzy? What matter if the stable boy be whipped? Does he not deserve it, falling asleep and letting thieves break in?"

"Nay. Nay. Enough, Neddie. You've no knowledge of what you say—no right to set blame——" Peg broke off abruptly. How explain to Neddie? Neddie who was no more than a baby. Neddie who, thanks be to Heaven, knew nothing as yet of crowns and thrones and plotting.

She turned her face away. "Let me tidy you, little brother, before you go down to table," she suggested, picking up a hairbrush. "Must your topknot always look like a wind-blown haycock?" She straightened his tunic and removed a top, a bit of sticky almond paste and a snail in its shell from his pockets, and then quietly she told him, "The flogging will bring pain, no matter where the blame lies. Think, Neddie, what of last winter when you wept with earache? Think upon your own hurt. Would you have wished for a staring crowd to gape and mock?"

Neddie's hand flew to the side of his head, and he winced reminiscently. " 'Twas only you I wished close, you and a poultice," he admitted. "And though I've no remembrance of weeping—at most no more than very little—'twould have been uncommon mean for any one to gawk." He was silent for a thoughtful moment. "Perchance, I shall stay up here with you after all," he announced then reluctantly. "Though what our uncle will say, I cannot guess—and should I truly stay, will you play soldiers with me?"

Peg promised.

When Neddie had run down to the Great Hall, she went to the window. Below, revelry was on again. A dozen wine butts had been broached in the middle of the courtyard. Two whole oxen were roasting in a pit. The jugglers were tossing a hundred balls again, like a drift of gold bubbles. The King's jesters were at their foolery once more. Peg could hear the tinkle of the silly little bells that waggled on their poppy-bright pointed caps and on the turned-up toes of their velvet shoes.

She could hear the lively banter, the coy shrieks, the scuffling as blowsy scullery maids were chased into a corner for a kiss or fought over for dancing partners. But above all the merrymaking, another sound rang in her ears.

As though the echo of his pain and terror were actually floating up to her, she could hear the sobs of the little hostler boy who, when the holiday was over, would feel a leather strap curl cruelly around his legs and loins. As clearly, she could hear the stretch and crack of his thumb joints as he hung on the barrack wall.

When the sobbing grew so real to her that she wanted to clap hands to ears to shut out its dreadfulness, Peg snatched her cloak and in a panic ran down the porter's stair and out into the courtyard.

Young Edward! She must seek him at once, for all the trembling of her legs under her. But where to waylay him? By the keep gate? Might he pass there once the noon meal was done inside?

She waited for him with what little courage she owned oozing fast. When he came out at last, he was no longer the glad eager boy she had turned eyes away from at breakfast.

His face was sulky, furious. Every drawn-up inch of him bespoke an arrogant Prince bent on full vengeance for the injury done him.

Knowing a far greater fright than when she had slipped a halter around Gweno's neck, Peg dropped a hasty curtsey. "A moment if you please, Your Highness," she stammered. "May I have speech with you?"

Young Edward shrugged impatiently. "Speech? And concerning what?" he wanted to know ungraciously.

"Concerning—concerning—concerning Gweno, Your Highness."

"So, you be sorry for me, as is everyone else?" Young Edward's short rude laugh gave away his chagrin, his bitter disappointment. "Save your pity, coz. I've no time for it."

He would have pushed past Peg, her sympathy salt to his hurt, but she dared to reach out and put a hand on his arm. "Stay! Hear me out, pray do. I be here to beg a favor. Will you not persuade our Uncle Richard to a change of heart? A calling to a halt of the flogging that he has commanded? Please! Please! I ask it most earnestly. What matter that the hostler lad slept last night away? 'Twas no sentry post he stood. No affair of life and death, that weariness of his. Would you whip a babe for so small a misdeed as the sleepy nodding of its head?"

Young Edward pulled free. "The matter stands. And none of it your concern that I can see. So let me pass, if it please you."

"Nay! You shall listen!" Peg's voice faltered and then she rushed on, recklessly. "What say if I declare it fault of mine alone, that your colt be gone? Mine, and no other's, that your Yule pleasure be spoilt? For 'twas I who stole Gweno. Not the hostler lad, I tell you—I, alone——"

"You?" Incredulously, Young Edward searched Peg's guilty face. "You? A likely tale, coz! And let me make it clear that I be in poor humor for jesting."

"But I speak the truth. Believe me! Believe me! My oath upon it."

Peg's confession spilled out, incoherently. "I rose at dawn. Made my way to the stable—turned your colt free at the edge of the moor. How else to act, knowing what I did? 'Twas to save you from a murdering—your death, had the colt been saddled. Listen to me well. Gweno would have thrown you at first mounting. He be a Killer—girthed. And you would have lain dead—dead! I heard it bandied so by His Grace of Gloucester's grooms. Heard it at the Feathers' Inn yard, where Neddie and I halted on our journey up from London."

"Be you daft?"

Young Edward's blue eyes smoked. With a twist of Peg's wrist that made her catch her lips between her teeth, he pulled her out of the boisterous crowd that swarmed the court-yard and shoved her on a bench against the wall. "How dare you, coz? How dare mouth such wicked babblings?" He gave her arm another twist. "You know full well who gave me Gweno. You know as well as I who had him fetched from London for me. And yet you have the gall to speak such lies?"

"Why not? All the more, rather, for that knowing." Wildly, Peg burst out with the truth. "Our uncle be vile. Vile, I say! An old story to me, his treacherous ways. Has no one ever told you of my father, brought to an end in the Tower? No one made it clear to you why Neddie and I must sit as beggars at your table?"

Young Edward reddened. "Where else but the Tower for traitors?" he countered haughtily. "I ask you to name a better place. And as to your stupid lies, have a care, coz. Spread them, and you'll be woeful sorry——"

The words trailed away. Young Edward's angry outraged eyes lost some of their assurance, some of their arrogance, as they stared at Peg's blanched face and at her mouth. It was trembling now, for all her brave burst of words.

Curious, a sudden unease welling in him; he wondered why he wanted to ask so many questions all at once? Granted that he did put them to her, would he wish truly to have them answered?

The wondering was uncomfortable. He was relieved to hear a hail from across the courtyard. Richard Pole was calling out, pushing a way through the merrymaking. When he reached the bench, he doffed his cap and gave a knee bend to Young Edward, a bow to Peg.

"So, here you be, Your Highness. Will you join the

games in the barrack hall? Your men-at-arms have sent me seeking you. They've halted their wrestling bouts, waiting your award of prizes. Shall we go along?"

"Nay."

Again Peg caught desperately at Young Edward's sleeve. "A promise from you first. Say yes! Say yes!" She turned imploringly to Richard Pole then as Young Edward pushed her away. "You be a friend to His Highness, Master Pole. A good friend. Make him hark to me. He must—he must!"

Struggling against tears, Peg poured out her story again. When she had finished, Richard Pole refused to be drawn into argument with Young Edward concerning its truth or falseness.

"There be time aplenty for pro and con some other day," he declared. "I agree with Mistress Margaret here. 'Tis the hostler boy who needs a hand at the moment. She's popped him into hot water and no mistake. Why not free the boy? Small wonder Mistress Margaret be troubled. There's little pleasure in thought of a flogging."

"And have I said there was? But let my cousin learn a lesson. 'Twill do her good! She'll ponder twice next time before she meddles. And for all I care she may weep her eyes out. Snivel herself into a puddle and drown. A liar, that's what she be. A black rotten liar. And a thief into the bargain, making off with Gweno."

"Come! Cool off, Your Highness. A halt to name-calling, there be a lady present. And if you'll not grant Mistress

Margaret a favor, what of one for me? Speak out to His Grace. Have an end put to the whipping. No need to spill all the whys and wherefores of your asking either. Let His Grace put it down to Christmas—an overflowing of good will towards men on your part."

"Christmas! And a fine one for me, with Gweno gone. That wretched boy shall take his flogging, I tell you."

Richard Pole shrugged. "Chances are I waste my breath arguing against such stubbornness as yours, my friend, but what say to this proposal—how's for a longbow match between us to settle the matter?" He put a persuasive arm around Young Edward's shoulder. "Be a good fellow. Take me on. And should you out-shoot me, let the flogging stand, if that be your pleasure. Have the hostler lad whipped to heart's content. But mind you, should the shoe be on the other foot, I ask your word that the lad go free. 'Tis up to you, so speak out. The stakes strike you as fair? And you'll agree?"

Young Edward hesitated. "Nay. I——"

"Ho! You turn a cold shoulder, eh? And why is that? Be there some doubt on your part, Your Highness, as to whose arrow will wing truest to our target if we set it up?"

"Doubt? Never! You'll see who wins. A plague upon you for your interference, but have it as you will. The wager holds. And the sooner settled between us, the better. I shall see you on the morrow. An hour before dusk at the sundial oak."

Before Young Edward strode off then, he tossed a last

angry contemptuous word to Peg. "Lucky for you, coz, that I be no talebearer. You'd get short shrift in certain quarters! And be glad upon your knees too that you were born a wench. A boy, and you'd take a pummeling from me. And one that you'd not forget in a hurry, let me tell you."

Chapter Five: AN AZURE ARROW

"The king is sickly——"
Richard III, Act I, SCENE 1.

That night as she made ready for bed, Peg pondered long and unhappily upon Young Edward. A most puzzling boy, to be consumed with pity one day for a broken-winged bird, steel-hearted the very next toward a wretched hostler lad. There was no fathoming him. With a sigh, Peg finished the plaiting of her hair and then set about covering Young Edward's thrush from the cold.

Neddie, bursting with a sudden interest that was born largely of a wish to put off his own bedtime as long as possible, protested vehemently against the little bird being tucked away without something offered it in the way of an especially cheery good-night.

"Poor songless thing. Fancy passing Christmas Day shut in a cage. Think how dreary for him, alone up here in this cold stone chamber. Talk to him for a bit, why don't you, Peg? Or better yet, why not sing to him?"

"Sing? In the middle of the night?"

"Please, Peg. Let him hear a chirp or two at very least if

it be too late for a true trilling. 'Twould be but kind. Did ever see so sad a bird? How he must miss his friends! Larks. Robins. Finches. All the others. Could you not cheer him the least bit? Won't you try?"

"And if I say 'yes' will you climb into bed at once, and close your eyes?"

The bargain was struck. When Neddie had settled himself on his pallet, his lead soldiers ranged in battle order on the quilt, his silver cart clutched tight, Peg puckered her lips. "Tweet, tweet, tweet. Tweet——"

The thrush, dropping dejectedly in a corner of the cage, had no answer for her.

"Try again, do, Peg!"

"Nay, Neddie. Enough is enough. I be weary—and—and my head is near to splitting for some foolish reason or another."

"But you will, all the same, won't you, Peg? Please, once more?"

Obediently, though with little heart for it, Peg puckered her lips again. "Tweet, tweet," she coaxed. "Tweet, tweet."

Her second effort to cheer the thrush was as vain as her first. She was more than ready to refuse Neddie's demand for a third attempt, when all at once, with its lackluster eyes taking on a hint of brightness, the thrush cocked an inquiring head.

"So, you choose to listen, do you, little fledgeling? Good. We are to be friends, then?"

The thrush stirred and actually gave a peep of its own. An

uncertain peep, and far from a happy one, but at least it was better than none at all.

"You see, Peg? I told you so!" Neddie popped up from his pillow triumphantly. "He wanted someone to talk to. He was lonesome. Your chirping was splendid! Don't stop. Chances are the thrush thinks you every bit as jolly as any wren he ever knew."

"Perchance. But if he be a good sensible bird and well-brought up, he knows as well as you that he must wait until morning for further chatting with me. You heard what I said, Neddie? Then off to sleep this very instant. Not another word."

Peg spread her petticoat over the cage and blew out the candle that stood on the oak chest. With another peep no more spirited than its last, the thrush put its head deep into its white breast feathers, resigned to making the best of another night in its prison.

Neddie's lashes fell on his rosy chubby cheeks.

Peg, alone, stayed awake.

The chapel bells rang out the hour of midnight. One o'clock. Two. Even then Peg was tossing and turning in her bed wondering fearfully what the morrow held.

Breakfast, when she went down to it, heavy-eyed and apprehensive, was much as it had been the day before. Princess Beth, in the absence of her late-sleeping parents, was in charge of her brothers and sisters. One minute she was gently correcting their table manners. Another, she was quietly but firmly ending a dispute over a jam pot. The next, she was picking up little Bridgit and holding her over her shoulder to pat up a windy bubble of mush and milk.

She had a gracious welcoming good-morning for Peg and a kind preoccupied smile. Young Edward on his part chose to ignore his cousin as Peg dropped her curtsey and took a seat at the foot of the table.

The slight was deliberate. And Peg had reddened painfully under it, as Richard Pole observed from what was evidently his customary place next to Beth. When he had finished his own meal he pushed away from the table and strolled over to her. "I find I have need of an arrow vane for the tipping of one of my shafts, Mistress Margaret," he stated casually. "Will you join me in search of a quill along the river bank? A good chance for you to glimpse the countryside, it strikes me. It be new to your eyes, I take it?"

"Entirely so, Master Pole. And a treat indeed for me to walk out." Peg's face glowed, and then clouded. "Speak honestly," she whispered with a quick glance at Young Edward. "I shan't mind the truth. Will you not be frowned upon for sharing company with me? I be in sore disgrace, remember."

"A fig for His Highness and those sulks of his. They'll pass; I know him well. So what say to a meeting at the outer gatehouse when you be done here? But mind you cloak yourself well. This northern cold bites deep."

Richard Pole had a bow for Peg when he left her, and before he sauntered out of the Great Hall, a last laughing intimate word or two with Princess Beth. Beth of the blood royal. Beth as flaxen-haired, as blue-eyed as Young Edward.

Beth, so pretty and gentle. So given to books and to learning.

Peg, darting little side glances at her cousin, remembered wistfully the leather-bound folios that Beth had exclaimed over so delightedly and passed around the board so proudly on Christmas Eve. They had been lately printed by that certain Master Caxton whose magical press was set up at the sign of the Red Pale in London. And Edward of England, ever generous and prodigal in his furthering of arts and letters, had opened his purse wide and bought a great, rich stack of them for her. A Yule treasure indeed: Legends of the Round Table, The Daring Deeds of Godfrey of Bolynge, The Story of Troilus, the witty, laugh-provoking history of Reynart the Foxe, Canterbury Tales.

To Peg it had seemed a rare privilege even to have fingered their covers, but Master Pole, she recalled, had been wondrously fortunate. Sitting next to Beth, he had shared the turning of every page with her, his quiet face alight, his eyes shining. Their heads had been close. Their hands touching. Their eager companionable chatter setting them apart in a delightful world all their own. A royal princess and her squire——

With an impatience rare to her, Peg jogged Neddie's elbow. "Hurry!" she urged sharply. "Must you stuff yourself to bursting? What! Three buns already, and you're reaching for another? Nay. And no more honey either. Hurry, I say! Do you think I have all day to wait?"

She rushed Neddie through the wiping of his sticky mouth and fingers, the making of proper bows to his cousins, and then she flew out of the hall and up the stairs for her cloak.

Breathless and vastly relieved at the sight of him, she joined Richard Pole at the gatehouse. When they were let pass by a sentry, he led the way to the river bank below. Scrambling and slipping, they took a rough faint path that plunged down the side of a wooded glen. Icy spray from a legion of white tumbling waterfalls blew against their faces. The humped knotted roots of tall firs and clumps of frost-burnt brakes tripped them. Briar and thorn bushes clawed at their clothes. Their breath hung frozen before them.

Reaching the river bank, they searched along it fruitlessly. The only feathers they came upon were of owl and hawk, and Richard Pole passed them by without second glance.

Leaving the glen behind them, they made for a stretch of open moor. After a moment's hunt, Richard Pole spied a sleek gray quill lying on the turf. "Here, we have it!" he exclaimed. "The very find I had in mind. A goose feather, and from a wing, at that. Cast an eye on it, Mistress Marga-ret. 'Tis as oily and smooth as they come. And bound to a shaft, 'twill give as sure and sweet a flight as ever archer could ask. You'll see! I've won from Young Edward already."

"Be you certain?" Peg's eyes were a trifle dubious. "Not that I doubt your skill, Master Pole, but truth to tell I've heard it said that His Highness pulls a far longer bow than one might imagine possible for his age."

"True. A lad uncommon strong in the arms and blessed with eyesight second to none, regardless of his years. But, seeing that he has been outshot before, why not again?"

There was nothing boastful about Richard Pole's question, and Peg found herself enormously cheered by his quiet assurance. The morning became surprisingly brighter. She even began to feel hungry and was more than glad when Richard Pole stopped by a little stone hut that stood staunch and solitary in the middle of the wide frozen wind-swept moor and asked her if she could do with a bite of lunch.

"This be a crofter's hut," he explained. "And whether the shepherd bides at home or be gone tending his flock, we are free to enter. A rule of the moor—and I have supped and warmed myself here more than once."

He gave a loud halloo and then pushed back the greasy hides that served as door to the hut and ushered Peg inside.

A turf fire smouldered on the stone hearth. A slow blue spiral of earthy-smelling smoke was being drawn up the hole that had been cut out for it in the low thatched roof.

Richard Pole lifted the lid of an iron pot that swung on a crane over the fire, stirred a moment, and ladled out two wooden bowls full of thick barley broth. Setting them down on a rough-hewn bench, he poked in the hearth ashes and pulled out a newly-baked oat cake which he broke into meticulously even halves.

After that, he searched in his pocket for a copper coin, laid it on the hearth for his absent host, and bade Peg seat herself.

"Here be a spoon, mistress. Dip in."

Peg obeyed eagerly, but the broth was hot, and while she

sniffed the good steam and blew on her spoon she ventured to make a word or two of conversation.

"You live here all the year, Master Pole, in this bleak Border country?" she asked. "Ludlow is your home?"

"Nay. I claim Buckinghamshire as such. 'Tis where my parents dwell. Where our manor lies. And a spot more pleasing to me than any my eye has ever lighted on. I shall seek it out for good and all once my spurs be won. But for the nonce, I serve here as squire under Sir John Manning."

"A knight who sat at table Christmas Eve? He be tall? Hawk-nosed? Scarred with a sword slash from left temple clean to jaw? And wore equerry's livery of claret and gold?"

"You have him pat, mistress. And 'tis his long-time close friendship with my Lord Rivers that keeps him here."

"My Lord Rivers? And who be he, pray?"

"The name means naught to you?" Richard Pole looked vastly surprised.

Peg flushed. "I be a stranger to court circles, and have been for a long time, Master Pole."

"Your pardon. I had forgot. Shall I put you straight? Well then, and first off, my Lord Rivers, that is to say Sir Anthony Woodville, is not alone favorite brother to the Queen herself, but ranks second to none in their Majesties' favor. And because he be so polished and wise a man of learning, they have set him over Young Edward as tutor. More, he serves as guardian to the Prince whatever months they may be absent in London."

"My cousin stays on at Ludlow without his sire, his lady mother? He lives all his days at the castle?"

"For the most part. A move, you understand, to make him known and well thought of in these parts. The good will of the Border chieftans who dwell along the West Marches here means much to the Crown and ever has. The day might well come when Young Edward would find their loyalty more than a little handy."

"You mean when he is grown? When 'tis his turn to be King?"

"Aye. And as there be parlous times ahead, chances are the Prince will have need of every man Jack in the Kingdom to keep him seated firm on his throne."

Peg sipped her broth. "Tell me," she asked slowly, "this noble and eminent Lord Rivers of whom you speak, this brother to the Queen, this guardian over Young Edward, be he friend to my uncle, the Duke of Gloucester?"

Richard Pole crooked a shrewd eyebrow. "You find the adding of the score puzzling, do you, Mistress Margaret? Small wonder! No simple sum, let me tell you. But here's my own answer, whatever it be worth. Before all else, the word 'friend' should be forgot. Put it out of mind. For though there be no swords drawn between them at the moment, both Lord Rivers and His Grace have hand on hilt, waiting."

"Waiting? But for what, Master Pole?"

"For the King's cup and trencher work to take him off. For a last belly ache, a last liverish spell to finish him."

Richard Pole had put it matter-of-factly. A little silence

fell. Peg munched her oat cake and then, in a voice scarce louder than a whisper, she asked another question.

"Answer me this, Master Pole—you believed my story concerning Young Edward's colt?"

"Believed it?" Master Pole frowned consideringly. "Aye, after due reflection. 'Twas a wild, far-fetched tale and an ugly one, you'll admit. Yet how not accept it, seeing that you have no look of a liar about you, no air of foolish tongue-wagging wench bent upon mischief making? Beside all that, there be those grooms you spoke of to lend weight to your words. Methinks I know them. Miles Forrest might be one, readily enough. John Dighton the other. They have ridden up from London a score of times, the both of them, in attendance on his Grace of Gloucester's mounts. A rough pair of louts to my mind. And neither of them in too great favor round stables or barracks, I've observed."

"Then, if you believe me—and I thank you for your taking of my word, Master Pole—you see as clear as I what lies ahead for Young Edward? Oh, I wonder if you do! The horrid end awaiting my cousin? The cruel trickery, the loathsome plotting that will surely do for him, one way or other, be it today or tomorrow or the next—you see it, Master Pole?"

"You think me blind? But simmer down, Mistress Margaret, simmer down, that's my advice. No use to wring hands. No use to run carrying your story from camp to camp. And there be more than one pitched here at Ludlow Castle, as well you may have guessed. For, granted that you've done Young Edward one good turn, there's naught more to accomplish at the moment. So lie low, I say, and keep a close mouth. You be steeped deep enough in the sorry brew that cooks here. Leave the next play to men. This be no affair for a maid's dabbling. And trust me, your tale concerning Gloucester and his Christmas colt will reach pricked ears, though whose is neither here nor there for the while."

Richard Pole stood up abruptly. "A sorry subject, this one we've dwelt upon. Best to drop it. And if it please you, we shall take our leave, Mistress Margaret. On your feet! High time and then some that I hie me back to the castle and set about my arrow feathering."

Peg put down her wooden bowl and shook the oat-cake crumbs out of her lap. When they left the hut's snug smoky shelter, the cold struck harsh and marrow-chilling against them. Peg wrapped her cloak close. Richard Pole turned up the sheepskin-lined collar of his brown leather jerkin and tugged his quilled cap firmly down on his bright locks.

They climbed away from the moor with a raw bullying wind against them and reached the top of the castle hill with nothing more said between them, both to save their breath and because each was occupied with his own thoughts.

When they had passed the outer gatehouse, Richard Pole thanked Peg for her company and bowed a leave-taking. Peg swept him a curtsey in return, but as he walked away, she followed close at his heels. "The day hangs heavy," she confessed wistfully, when he turned to look back surprised. "My concern be grave, my thoughts dark, I've no liking to be alone. May I go along with you? Watch the fashioning of your arrow tip? The fletcher's craft be new to me, and one in which much of interest lies, I judge. Would I be in your way, Master Pole?"

"Not in the least degree. And more than welcome, if it pleases you to watch me at my labors."

Richard Pole's reply was mannerly enough, but as he crossed the courtyard and Peg trailed after him, she was wishing belatedly that she had let him strike off without her. How bold he must think her, she chided herself, hot-cheeked and flurried, how stupid, how tiresome a maid. In the first place, she had been invited to go walking only because Sir Golden Cap was kindly-natured and sorry for the tangle she had knotted with her rash meddling. Now she was imposing even further upon his pity, though she knew quite well that he would forget her very existence once his archery match with Young Edward was over.

No two ways about it. Of course she would be forgotten. A boy like Sir Golden Cap had so many other things to think about—hunting, hawking, fishing, tilting. Then, in any spare moments, there were those beautiful books of Princess Beth's to keep him enthralled.

Princess Beth, flaxen-haired Beth, blue-eyed Beth. An odd pang struck Peg, its sudden pain entirely mystifying. She put her hand to her bosom. That curious stab—had it come from so commonplace a cause as climbing uphill too rapidly? Not entirely convinced of it, she followed Richard Pole into a workshop that adjoined the barracks and armory.

Three or four men, seated at a workbench, were concerned with precise and delicate whittling. Another, buffer in hand, was polishing a finished bow, while a fellow worker twisted together the strands of hemp that would string it.

Richard Pole walked over to a quiver that hung on the wall and pulled out an arrow. "Cast an eye, mistress," he commanded Peg. "What say to this? 'Tis my pride and joy, I warn you, so mind you compliment it."

"You fashioned it yourself, Master Pole?"

"Aye. And 'tis cut from finest ashwood that knew the seasoning of a full twelve months."

Richard Pole ran his hand over the arrow. "A beauty, if I do say so. You mark how slender, how straight? And test its lightness, its even balance."

He handed Peg the arrow and while she examined it admiringly, he fetched a bucket of boiling water from a trivet that stood over a nearby charcoal brazier. "Now for the soaking of our goose quill. That be the first step in the shaping of a proper vane. But stand back, mistress, else you risk a scalding."

He let the quill float in the bucket until it was soft and pliable enough to suit him, and then he fished it out and wiped it dry with a bit of clean linen rag. Hands steady, eyes intent, he clipped it short and trim with the sharpest of knives and then bound it with a beeswaxed cord to his prized shaft.

When he had held it up and sighted along it half a dozen times to his complete satisfaction, he nodded to a row of dye pots that were set out on the long plank workbench. "Which color for my arrow, think you, Mistress Margaret? Make a choice. Purple? Russet? Or what of azure? A favorite hue of mine and one to bring me luck, mayhap, when I come against Young Edward."

"'Then settle upon it without further question, Master Pole. You could do no better."

Richard Pole selected a rabbit-hair brush from a number that were scattered on the bench. Dipping it into a dye pot he stroked along the ashwood shaft painstakingly and lovingly until it was colored blue as larkspur.

"How's that, Mistress Margaret? Not bad, eh? And now there remains but the shooting of it."

It was late that afternoon just as the pale winter sun began its early drop behind the castle towers that Young Edward stalked out of the keep. Taking his way to a private courtyard that was known as the King's Garden, he clanged an iron gate behind him and walked down a long narrow alleyway that was lined on either side with dark glistening holly and somber yew.

A mossy stump that served as pedestal for a sundial lay at the end of the alley's thyme-turfed path. Drawing the dagger that was thrust through his jeweled belt, Young Edward began to hack at its bark. Soon he had cut a circle only a little larger round than the buckle that clasped the three Prince of Wales plumes to his velvet cap. Inside it, he cut another, and with a quick flick, nicked a bull's-eye in the center, wiped his blade, returned it to its sheath and stepped back a good forty paces.

Then he unslung a bow from the quiver that hung at his right hip, abristle with peacock and goose and pigeon feather tips. He was flexing his bow for a practice shot when the gate clanged again, and Richard Pole and Peg came in sight.

Again, as he had at breakfast, Young Edward chose to ignore his cousin and her curtsey. With no more than the stiffest of bows to Richard Pole, he asked coldly, "You'll agree, will you, to four draws each?"

"As you wish, Your Highness."

"Then a toss for first try." Young Edward took a silk purse from his doublet, opened it and spun a gold coin on the turf. "Crown up, 'twill be mine," he announced curtly. "Down, and 'twill be yours."

He lost the toss. Richard Pole stepped forward to the forty-pace mark and unslung his bow. While Peg watched, her hopes now up, now down, her heart racing, he set himself square to the stump, left foot a little in advance of right, weight settling even, his tall, slight figure erect. With cool eyes narrowing, he sighted for the hacked-out target and made ready to draw, three fingers crooking under his bowstring, his arm and wrist stiff as steel.

Zi—ing!

Wha—ang!

The arrow that he had chosen for his first try was dyed as red as a cockscomb. Streaking through the air, it imbedded itself well inside the second circle, no more than a sixteenth of an inch from the bull's-eye.

Peg sucked in a deep audible breath. Richard Pole pulled

THREE MISSES AND BUT A SINGLE TRY LEFT.

another arrow from his quiver. Drawing it to the full length of its green shaft, he laid his whole body into the bow and let fly. Scarcely had it whizzed through the air and lighted on the target, grazing the red arrow, than he sent a yellow to crowd it. Three misses and but a single try left.

Peg clenched her hands into tight cold fists. Surely, now if ever, the moment had come for Sir Golden Cap's fourth arrow to prove itself. The azure beauty, straight-shafted, true-balanced, that he had saved until the last. Would its short smooth-trimmed tip lend it a steadier flight than those other arrows he had shot? Had the vanes of the green and the red and the yellow been over-long, ragged-edged, the least bit? Might that explain their slight but fatal drift in the wind that had begun to stir among the yew and holly trees?

Again, as Peg asked her silent questions, Richard Pole laid his body into his bow. The blue arrow sped to the target, only to impale itself the barest hair's-width closer to the bull's-eye than the three before it.

Lest she cry out her disappointment, her dismay, Peg clapped hand to mouth, as Richard Pole stepped back and made way for the Prince.

The troublesome wind played no favorites. Young Edward drew bow three times, and three times his arrows, veering lightly, buried their tips the same sixteenth of an inch from the bull's-eye as Richard Pole's.

For his last try, he dug his heels hard into the turf,

planted himself firmly and drew bow deliberately, its hemp cord taut along his jaw.

With a loud twang, the arrow winged free. Taking swift, sure flight, it pierced the exact center of the target. Thrusting deep into the mossy stump, it stuck fast and hung there, quivering, triumphant as a death shaft in the neck of a roebuck.

Chapter Six: UP, A RED ROSE!

"Oh bloody Richard!
Miserable England!"
Richard III, Act III, SCENE 4.

"I be sorry, mistress. Would I might have served you better." Sir Golden Cap walked to the oak stump and pulled out his arrows.

"The fault be none of yours, Master Pole . . ." Peg's little murmur died away.

Young Edward, finding the silence that followed as uncomfortable, as sharp-edged as the rising wind in the yews, took refuge in a taunt. "You wear an over-long face, cousin," he gibed. "Why not carry your grievance to our uncle himself, and see how you fare? Only try it—I dare you!"

"I be on my way to him this very moment, Your Highness." Quietly Peg had turned to the garden gate.

Young Edward stared unbelievingly. Richard Pole was equally as astonished. "A wise course you think, Mistress Margaret?" he queried. "It strikes me you be a very lion for courage."

"A lion? Ha, ha!" Young Edward burst out with a loud, scoffing laugh. "She'll be mincemeat, rather, when my uncle

87

be done with her. But what say, coz? You'll grant me leave
to accompany you to his chamber? A pity to miss the sport.
'Twill be rare and no mistake. A joke if a second flogging
should be commanded!"

He had the grace to color then, and to stop short under
Richard Pole's grave glance, but his head was in the air as
arrogantly as ever a moment later as he marched to the gate
and opened it for Peg with a mocking bow. The two of them
walked out of the King's Garden together in silence. The
sun had gone down. A gray chilly mist swathed the castle
turrets. The courtyard cobblestones glistened with damp.

At the entrance to the keep, a sentry sprang to attention,
blue-nosed with the cold, the filthy evil-smelling sheepskins
that wrapped him matted and curling with moisture. Salut-
ing Young Edward, he passed them through into the charge
of a halberdier who wore the Duke of Gloucester's silver
boar blazoned on his sleeve.

A long dusk-shadowed draughty passageway stretched
ahead of them empty and yet alive with the little stir, the
rustling whisper of the needlework figures on the tapestries
that billowed out from the stone walls.

When they were ushered into Crook-Back's chamber,
they found him alone. With his high-backed chair drawn
close to the hearth, a small table set up, he was dealing out
a pack of painted playing cards, picking up a scarlet knave
now and again, or a gold chevalier, and then coldly, precisely, covering them both with a purple king. Behind him
his shadow flickered on the wall.

Peg, having made a curtsey, edged to the far end of the hearth, her hands to the blaze. She was shivering, wordless. How to begin? What to say?

"Mistress Margaret has lost her tongue, uncle," Young Edward burst out without waste of time. "She craved a boon of you, but now, 'twould seem she lacks zest for it." He tossed a contemptuous glance at Peg. "Nor do I wonder! But speak, uncle, have I your ear? Then what say you to this scurrilous tale of hers? Did ever hear the like?"

Indignantly, wrathfully, Young Edward unburdened himself. "—were ever blacker lies spoken?" he wanted to know when he had come to the end. "I be ashamed to mouth them concerning you, uncle. And though her slandering be the worst of it, think on all the rest—my cousin's stupid meddling, her thievery. Think on it, uncle, Gweno gone! Gweno lost to me, thanks to her mischief-making."

Crook-Back heard Young Edward through, dealing his cards, picking them up and setting them down again in neat piles. A faint smile twisted his lips. A smile that was mildly rebuking. "Come now, come now, nephew. You deemed so wild a flight of fancy worthy of my notice? I thank you for your loyalty, but where be your common sense? Look upon the matter in its proper light. True, your colt is gone, but there'll be others. And as for your cousin's calumny against me, dismiss it from your mind. What be it, after all, but absurd and womanish phantasy?"

"Phantasy? Nay, she swears to it as true, uncle. True as day and night. And there be no persuading her otherwise."

For the first time Crook-Back's black unwavering eyes went to Peg. "Methinks the long journey from London proved overwearying to her," he observed to Young Edward as he sorted a handful of cards. "A hard rough ride for even the most seasoned of travelers. There be the cold to consider as well, and the damp of this bitter month. What more likely that they brought a rheum upon your cousin? A fever. A bout of light-headedness. 'Twould explain much."

Crook-Back picked a scarlet knave from his board and played it deliberately. "Dismiss the matter, nephew," he advised again. "Put it aside. 'Twas a fever my poor niece suffered, I tell you. That and nothing more drove her to the freeing of your colt, the loosening of her tongue in such soft-witted gabbling."

"You truly think it?" Young Edward's blue eyes spoke his lack of conviction and his uncertainty. "Then, if you say so, uncle— And do you hear, cousin? You stand in the clear, 'twould seem. Our uncle proves most lenient. I'd thank my lucky star, were I in your shoes!"

Peg, cringing by the fire, had no answer for him beyond a lift of her lashes and her quick beseeching glance.

Young Edward reddened as he had under Richard Pole's grave weighing eyes. Looking away quickly, he hesitated for a stubborn moment and then faced Crook-Back once again. "The stable boy—his flogging, his stringing-up-by-the-thumbs—it comes to mind, uncle," he brought out awkwardly. "Might his punishment be lessened, think you? Hardly just to let it stand, with my cousin here let off so light. Seeing 'tis the Christmas season in the bargain——"

"You'll grant a pardon, Your Grace? Oh, do! Do!" Peg had found her voice. She was begging now and fairly wringing her hands. "Let him go! The blame is mine. All mine. No slightest share be his."

Again Richard of Gloucester's dark gaze sought Peg. "You plead convincingly, niece," he remarked with his twisted smile. "The flogging shall be forgot along with all else that pertained to your fevered state." He turned to Young Edward. "Seek out the Captain of the Guard, nephew. Say 'tis my wish that earlier orders be revoked. Have the boy sent back to his stable and his straw pile."

"At once, uncle. And my thanks!" Young Edward darted a glance at Peg. "I ben't over-fond of floggings," he admitted to no one in particular.

He was off then to the door, and Peg, dropping a curtsey, would have slipped away only too gladly if Richard had not stayed her. "A moment, niece. Time, methinks, that you and I became better acquainted. And what better chance than now?"

He waited until Young Edward had gone, and then he laid down his cards and pushed the board away. "Stand closer, if it please you," he ordered coldly. "Let me have a look at you. But why so trembling? Why so harelike, so white of face, niece? You regret your slandering of me, perchance? Wish too late that such words as 'murderer' and the like had been choked back before you voiced them?"

He gripped Peg's shoulder until she winced and cried

out. "You be heeding closely, niece? I trust so, for I would speak of your brother at this point. I be told you hold deep affection for him—true? Heart-touching, such sisterly devotion! But take heed. For if you wish him well, if you but wish him the very continuance of his days, mind you set guard upon your tongue from henceforth on. Mind you stopper your ears, as well, and shutter your eyes. And for good measure, make certain that you keep well aloof from affairs that be none of your concern. You have listened well, as I bade you, niece? You grasp the import of my words? Then be gone. My say is said."

Richard of Gloucester's hand loosened on Peg's shoulder. He picked up his cards again, and somehow, blindly, Peg stumbled from the room.

Young Edward was waiting for her at the keep gate. "Stop a moment, coz." He barred her way as she tried to run past him. "I be sorry for my talebearing," he blurted. "Little did I think I had it in me to carry tales against a maid. 'Twas a loyalty toward our uncle that undid me—a rising of my gorge at the charge you laid against him."

"No need for further words, Your Highness—only let me pass, I beg you."

"Nay. Don't go, so turned against me, so out of sorts. I be sorry, I say. Aye, and what's more, willing even to forgive you Gweno's loss. One thing alone remains to settle——"

There was an odd persistency and an earnestness in the question that Young Edward asked then, holding fast to Peg's arm. "Answer me this, coz. You see for yourself now that it was indeed the cold, the long journey from London that addled your wits so strangely? The light-headed imaginings of a fever that took you to the Feathers' stable? And all of it was delusion, purest phantasy just as our uncle declared?"

"You heard it so, Your Highness. What more to add?"

"Then with matters cleared between us, shall we cry quits to our quarreling? You will let me be your friend once more?"

" 'Friend'? As you wish. I have few enough, to willingly scorn another."

Peg pulled away and ran. When she reached her chamber she threw herself on the bed, her heart beating hard and fast. Neddie. Neddie. Little innocent Neddie, who was all that she had in the world. And now his very life was the curb that Crook-Back had set upon her tongue. Never, never, would she dare utter another word against him. But had his warning come too late? What of Master Pole? He had spoken of pricked ears? Had her rash confidences reached them already? Might they leak to Crook-Back? And what then if their source were laid at her door?

A clamor of bells put an end to surmise. Drearily, reluctantly, Peg roused herself to brush her hair and change into her shabby velvet dress.

Another Yuletide feast. Another revel. To a fanfare of trumpets, the King and the Queen walked to their däised chairs in the Great Hall, Edward in cloth-of-gold tunic, a mastiff at his side, Elizabeth in wine velvet, her hooded falcon leashed to her wrist.

When the games and dancing began, Young Edward promptly sought out Peg and proposed himself as her partner for the evening. "You will wear my favor, be my lady?" He asked it with far less than his usual arrogant self-assurance and looked vastly pleased when Peg let him pin a tinsel and ribbon rosette on her shoulder. "I be glad that by-gones be by-gones," he told her. "I own to a liking for you, coz. I shall speak to my father concerning you, that your stay at Ludlow may be lengthened. Beth and Cecily and the others find you pleasing, too. Will you stay on with us? We shall have sport, the lot of us."

The striking up of harps and gitterns, the clear trill of a flute from the minstrel gallery called something to his mind then. "A pox upon me, I had almost forgot! What of my moor bird? My thrush, you have coaxed a warble from it as yet?"

"Nay. No more than a peep, Your Highness. But have patience. A song will come, I promise. Your bird has but need of time to forget its hurt, its fright. Time to learn the meaning of a cage."

All the while that Peg chattered on about the thrush her eyes were anxiously seeking out Richard Pole.

Ah, there he was, halfway across the hall, and partner to the Princess Beth as was to be expected. Little hope that he would stray from her side for even a single minute.

Peg had just begun a game of snapdragon with Young Edward when to her great relief Sir Golden Cap sauntered over at last and stood watching the fun. It was Peg's turn to snatch a raisin from a bowl of flaming brandy. She reached for it hastily, clumsily, and then ignoring the smart of her burnt fingers, and while Young Edward pushed forward eager and laughing for a turn of his own, she caught hold of Master Pole's tunic sleeve. "I must see you—have words with you," she whispered urgently. "You will meet me early on the morrow at the crofter's hut, as soon as it be daylight? Please! You'll come?"

Richard Pole eyed her sharply and pulled her a little to one side. "What's up? You stirred a hornet's nest this afternoon, Mistress Margaret?"

Before Peg could answer, a merry rough throng surging toward the snapdragon bowl was pushing them apart and she had no more than a brief agreeing nod from Sir Golden Cap for her comfort. Would he remember her plea when morning came? Would he think it worth rousing from a warm bed at so unlikely an hour as dawn? A miracle if he did! And would the evening never draw to a close?

It was midnight before the revel was over, with the King and Queen yawning themselves to bed, minstrels muting their harps, jesters ceasing their foolish capering, candles guttering, torch-flares palely dying.

At sunrise the castle was a-rumble with snores when Peg tiptoed down the porter's stair and out of the courtyard. The wide moor she sought was all but deserted. Once she heard a distant shepherd piping to his dog. Once she passed a peasant bound for market, his brown cloak the color of the frosted bracken that crackled under his clogs.

Upon reaching the crofter's hut, and trusting that its owner would prove absent with his flock, she called out timorously. Richard Pole, hallooing from inside, held back the ragged hides from the doorway.

He was not alone. A knight, whom Peg recognized as Sir John Manning, was seated on the hearth bench. A furred mantle dropped from his shoulders, a gold chain hung round his neck, his legs were clothed in soft leather boots to his thighs, but there was the look of a soldier about him, and of a man more at ease in armor than in the richness of court attire.

"Enter, Mistress Margaret." Richard Pole bowed and doffed his cap. "There be no need for introductions? Then will you draw to the fire while my lord here puts a word to you?"

"I shall move to the point swiftly, mistress." Sir John's eyes, from under the shaggy brows that met over his hawk nose, bored into Peg's. "A firm conviction of mine that this matter of Gloucester's grooms, the steed that they stabled at the Feathers' inn yard on Yule Eve, should rightly be carried to Lord Rivers and to various other Council members. But first, you swear that the tale be true? You'd take oath upon it if called before them?"

"Nay! Never!"

Peg flung it out in terror. "Forget that ever I spoke, my lord, and you as well, Master Pole. 'Twas naught but—but phantasy, all of it. Phantasy, I say. A phantasy bred of my weary journey. Bred of fever—of light-headedness."

"A phantasy? Why such over-fondness for the word?" Sir John turned to Richard Pole. "Be the maid a simpleton?" he demanded. "Faith, 'twould sound so, and my coming here to question her a wild-goose chase."

"Not so fast, Sir John. Contain yourself. Search the maid's face. When was fright writ plainer? And methinks she'd run from us in another moment if her legs but held her up."

As he spoke, Richard Pole drew Peg to the hearth bench. "Bide a while by the warmth, Mistress Margaret," he suggested. "And how's for spooning up a bit of porridge? A hospitable pot, this one hanging here. I take it you've not broken fast as yet this morning?"

He tossed a fresh square of peat onto the slow-burning, smoky fire and set a wooden bowl in Peg's hands. He waited until she had swallowed a few spoonfuls of the porridge, and then he asked quietly, "You be in fresh trouble? Why not spill it? How else secure our aid? Let's have it."

Peg's eyes filled. "You be kind, Master Pole. Most kind."

"Then, if you think so, why not trust Sir John and me? Why not speak out freely?"

"Only for reason that—that——" Peg's voice shook. "Only for reason that I dare not, Master Pole. A loose tongue would but prove a further undoing. Would but plunge me deeper into misfortune. Worsen my state most fearfully. And 'twould be Neddie who suffered even more than I—my Neddie who would bear the brunt."

"So, a turn of the screws, eh?" Again, Sir John's sharp eyes bored into Peg's. "Your uncle has mouthed a warning, a threat?" He followed his shrewd guess with a short laugh. "And thus stoops lower, even than I had thought. My apologies, little maid. You had good reason and more, for crying down so heinous a tale. And I promise you that Lord Rivers or any other shall hear it from me without faintest hint as to its source. My oath upon it. Think you I'd chance the risk of bogging you deeper in the muck where your uncle shapes his slimy plots? No fear. God's Mother, how monstrous a fellow he be! Never was such infamy."

"But who pays heed, my lord?" Peg cried her question passionately. "Who in all the kingdom cares? Will no one, no one, ever step forward to put end to his wickedness? Oh, if I were but a man! If a woman could but wield a sword!"

Sir John exchanged a dry smile with Master Pole as he stood up and wrapped his cloak around himself. "Take heart, mistress. Before I bid you good-bye let me tell you that there be more than a few honest Englishmen who but bide their time—your humble servant among them, I might add—and all of us waiting for a clock to strike. Tell me, have ever heard the name of Henry Tudor?"

"You speak of the Earl of Richmond, my lord? I know naught of him except that he dwells in exile and has long been out of favor with the Crown, though the whys and wherefores lie beyond my ken."

"Natural enough. A devious story, his, and one that began its unfolding when you were yet unborn, mistress. But mark his cognomen well. 'Twill spell Nemesis one day to

Gloucester, if I be not mistaken. Let's hope for it. For exiled though he be in Brittany, his every wakening thought, his every dream, centers upon his native England. 'Twill be a battle to the death between him and Richard, should Richard dare usurp the throne once Edward's gone."

"A grievance lies between them, my lord?"

"Aye, and their bone of contention the rights of the House of Lancaster against the rights of the House of York. So I say it again, mistress. Mark the name Tudor well. And hark for that certain cry, 'Up with the Red Rose, down with the White!' You'll hear it, I promise."

"And your stand, Sir John, should His Grace of Richmond's day truly come?"

"With all other men of honor, Mistress Margaret. Whatever our former allegiance, wherever it lay, with Red Rose or White, there will be but a single issue once the Tudor steps on English soil. The unhorsing of Crook-Back. The kingdom's riddance of him, let the weapon at hand be what it may."

Chapter Seven: BLUE VELVET AND ERMINE

"Does this news hold of good King Edward's death?
. . . Then, masters, look to see a troublous world."
Richard III, Act II, scene 3.

The holidays were over. The Christmas Candle, shaped
in the likeness of the Holy Lamb, had been snuffed out.
The Yule Log was no more than a white ash on the hearth.
The garlands of holly and bay, fir and ivy, had dried and
shriveled against the stone walls of the Great Hall. Twelfth
Night saw them dragged down and burnt, flaring in a
brief crackling blaze, and then giving up their pungent
ghosts.

The world outside the castle lay deep in snow. Snow that
was white and pure on the moor, marred with nothing more
than the tracks of a hare or fox or badger. Snow that car-
peted the courtyard with soiled icy slush.

Up in the west tower where the Royal Chamber looked
out toward the dark stern Welsh mountains, King Edward
was passing more of his days than not upon a bed made soft
with goose down and sheepskins and quilted velvets. Restlessly, incessantly, for all the agues, the head pains he suffered, he spoke of nothing but London, London. What mat-

ter, snow and sleet and wind? Blocked roads, overflowing rivers? Nothing should keep him away any longer from the city that he loved so much.

On the day when he was at last carried out of the court-yard in a curtained litter, Young Edward and Lord Rivers waved him good-bye from the castle's parapets. They waved, as well, to the Queen and to Beth and Dickon and Cecily, riding off, hooded and furred upon their white palfries. Waved to a second litter and to a third that carried Katherine and Anne and Little Bridgit and their nursemaids.

But it was Young Edward alone who waved to Richard of Gloucester. His Grace had taken the lead of the long procession, a black velvet riding-mantle lined with fox pelts wrapped close around his humped shoulders, his dark eyes expressionless in the shadow of a fur-edged hood.

As he rode away Peg, watching from her window-slit, drew a deep breath of thankfulness. No one had suggested that she and Neddie join the cavalcade to London. In all the concern over the King's health, the stir of travel preparations, they had been passed over, ignored. That they should stay on indefinitely at Ludlow Castle seemed to be taken for granted.

And what a mercy to have it so! Peg's gratitude was boundless.

She and her uncle under separate roofs. Crook-Back miles and miles away. And now, perchance, he would forget all about her, forget about Neddie. Leave them out, once and for ever, from his plotting and scheming.

Peg was still lingering at her window-slit long after the royal procession had wound down the hill and was lost to sight. Below, in the courtyard, Richard Pole had begun a game of quoits with Young Edward. Looking down on him, Peg felt again the new strange pain in her breast. Sir Golden Cap had lingered unduly long, to her mind, over his fare-wells to Princess Beth when she rode away. Need there have been such a to-do about so small a thing as a leave-taking? Was a journey to London the same as a journey to the ends of the world? Not in the least! And, oh how small, how white Beth's hand, stripped of its riding gauntlet, that Sir Golden Cap might press lips to it. Ah me—ah me——

The short wintery days that followed King Edward's de-parture succeeded one another as quietly, as regularly as the snow that never ceased to fall from leaden skies. For Peg, and for all the other women gathered in the Great Hall, there was weaving and spinning, endless quilting and hem-ming and embroidery to pass the time.

For Young Edward and Richard Pole there were lessons with Lord Rivers. A globe to turn in search of strange seas and distant lands. Mathematical problems to solve. A knowledge of the stars to be gleaned. The mastery of Latin and Greek and of the French tongue. A reading of philoso-phies and poetry. Nor could music be neglected. Hour upon hour must be spent in practice of choral and plain song.

When all of that lay behind them, there was barrack life to enter into. A dexterity to be gained in the use of sword and lance and bow. A perfecting of horsemanship. A degree of skill to be won at the practical tasks of repairing the steel and leather trappings of a battle-charger, the hammering of a dented casque into shape, or the forging of new links for any one of a dozen pieces of armor.

The long evenings, as well, fell into a pattern. First, a good supper of mutton and brawn and salt fish, honey and bread, and of a hot pudding rich with suet and nuts and raisins and spice. Afterwards, chair drawn close to the hearth, Lord Rivers would quaff a tankard of ale in company with my Lord Grey, a stepson to the King, and left behind to share guardianship of the castle with him. On occasion, Young Edward and Master Pole would discuss the affairs of the world with them or listen to the essays and poetry that they read aloud, but more often than not, they would set up a chess board.

Now and again they invited Peg to take a turn, with Young Edward playing the part of teacher and quoting profoundly from a Christmas book that Beth had left behind, *The Game and Play of Chess.* It was one of Master Caxton's publications.

For Neddie the evenings held a round of lively games. Sometimes it was hide-and-seek with one or a dozen of the castle children. Sometimes tag, up and down the long corridors. Sometimes a noisy knocking-down of nine pins. Sometimes a cracking of nuts on the hearth, a romp and tumble with the stretched-out hounds. And always, when bedtime came, an indignant protest and a reluctant sleepy-eyed stumbling up the stone stairs, a shivering dive under his quilts. Peg, tucking him in, bending down to kiss him good night, blowing out his candle, would tell herself, scarcely daring to believe it, that she and Neddie had at long last found a haven.

Make it so, kind Heaven! Make it so! She begged it in her prayers every night, kneeling on the icy floor, her teeth chattering, as she began them, only to end them earnestly and apologetically from under her warm bed quilts.

One morning when January had stretched into February, February into a bleak March, March into early undecided April, she woke to spring. Anyone could tell! Anyone would know! Having ventured for a walk down the hill to the river, Peg exclaimed joyfully at sight of a patch of rich red Shropshire earth showing under the melting snow. Too, there was the tinkle of breaking ice in the salmon and greyling pools. A bit of blue appearing bravely through a rift in the ragged wind-blown clouds.

On yet another day, she saw the swell of sap along the branches of a blackthorn hedge. Trefoil showed itself then, a clump here, a clump there. An eager up-thrust of reeds and grasses and lily pads was asserted in the water-meadows. Larch and ash offered their leafy embrace from every coppice.

In the Great Hall, green sallets of tender purslaine and cress were passed, purging away the winter's scurvy, ending the monotony of dried peas and pithy roots, and there was a brisk sweeping out of musty floor-rushes to make way for a fresh strewing of thyme and fennel.

On the very morning that Peg had been brave enough to strip off her linen shift and woolen petticoats and sponge herself all over from the wooden bucket of hot water lugged her by Susan Dow, she found a primrose on the river bank and heard a cuckoo's call. Spring indeed.

Soon, she knew, there would be mavis and goldfinch singing in the hedges, bunting and lark, turtledove cooing and the chirp of robin and sparrow. A thousand pities that Young Edward's thrush should be absent from the choral. And slothful of her, nay worse, unkind, that all the past months she had paid little or no attention to it beyond its feeding and the cleaning of its cage.

In the beginning she had been too unhappy, too beset with fear to care whether or not she could bring back its song with an encouraging trill of her own. Later, when Crook-Back had gone and the snowy quiet days had offered her peace of mind, the little bird had proved woefully uninterested in singing lessons. Would it ever make an effort to find its lost warble? Would it ever put forth more than an occasional tentative peep-peeping? Doubting it, Peg had lost interest, except for a fleeting regret now and then that her painstaking bandaging had been in vain. The thrush still dragged a wing. It would never fly again. Poor bird. Poor unnatural feathered thing. Listening to the song all around her, Peg knew a fresh pity for the thrush. Once more she would do what she could for it. Might it prove more apt a pupil if she fetched it out of her cheerless cold chamber into the open sunlight? If it could hear the twittering that came now from every tree and bush and hedge?

She asked Young Edward's opinion that evening and together they decided on a larger cage for the thrush before all else. Having braided one of willow whips from the river, they hung it in the courtyard where Young Edward and Richard Pole had shot their arrows. The King's Garden faced south and west, cupping whatever sun there was, and all through the green mat of ivy that covered its stone walls there was a lacing of little shreds of straw and lint and twigs to give away the secret of a multitude of nesting places.

In a week's time, whether because of the sun or because of the companionable twittering round about him, the thrush began to find a joy in its days. Began to twitter on its own accord. Began to sing a little. And then to sing a little more.

"My warbler should be yours by rights, coz. I shall give it to you. 'Tis you who deserve its song, not I," Young Edward declared generously on an afternoon when he and Peg were sitting on a bench in the sundial court, listening to the liquid trill that poured so freely from the thrush.

"And if I took you at your word? Ran off with your bird? What would you say then, Your Highness?"

Peg's eyes held a teasing smile and Young Edward laughed outright. "You know me well, coz! I would act the prince, you may be certain, and utter royal command that you bring it back, and at once, upon pain of severest punish-

ment. A happier arrangement if we declared joint owner-
ship, mayhap?" He laughed again. "And with you as cage-
cleaner to my thrush, coz, and I to be concerned solely
with its music."

He held out a sprig of cress and a few millet seeds to his
bird. "Come," he coaxed, "come, perch upon my hand and
give me another roundelay."

With a hop and a lopsided flutter of wings the thrush
obeyed and after a peck or two was bursting its white throat
in another soaring sweet trill.

There was a little concert in the sunny garden every day
after that until late April, when a horseman, galloping at
top speed into the castle courtyard, put a sudden end to
Young Edward's interest in so trifling a toy as a tame
thrush. The fagged travel-stained messenger was the bearer
of a scroll announcing the death of the King.

"A fever did for him, a chill," Lord Rivers told Young
Edward. "And now, with him lying in state at the palace,
your gracious mother, the Queen, desires your presence at
once. She and your brother and sisters be desolate, sore-
hearted indeed, from the words her pen has writ. It be
your duty to go to her with all speed."

Lord Rivers knelt then and held out the hilt of his drawn
sword. "And now my homage, Your Majesty."

"Homage?"

"What else, to my sovereign?"

"A pity, my lord, that I must lose a parent to gain a
crown. Would it might have been otherwise. I had love for

my father—love in abundance——" Young Edward struggled to swallow the lump in his throat and to banish a threat of tears. His yellow head went into the air. "I shall strive mightily to be worthy of my kingdom," he vowed. "Trust me, my lord, I shall try with all my heart to fill my sire's empty place."

There was a swift formulating of plans in the next few days. Lord Rivers, as Young Edward's guardian, sent the Queen's messenger posthaste back to London bearing word that her monarch son would soon be with her.

Sir John Manning, elevated to the post of Captain of the Garrison, was to remain at the castle. Lord Rivers himself and Lord Grey, borrowing the services of Richard Pole as their squire for the journey, and as a youthful companion to Young Edward, would escort the new king on his immediate ride south. No more than half a dozen henchmen were to attend them on the long and arduous journey. For the furthering of a swift departure, and rapid traveling, they would proceed in as unencumbered a manner as possible. The pomp of royal retinue, the blare of trumpets, the waving of banners could wait until the Lord Mayor of London and a host of loyal subjects welcomed their sovereign at the gates of his city.

To Peg's surprise she found herself and Neddie included in the small hurriedly-arranged group of travelers. Lord Rivers had proffered a suggestion for their future that was too practical to be refused.

Would Peg consent to take up lodgings with his good

and long-time friend Master Caxton, the printer of Westminster? And if her answer were yes, what more convenient opportunity than now for the journey to London?

Why not accept without second thought? The need for a change of abode was obvious, surely? Mistress Margaret realized for herself that with the Queen and the Princesses, Dickon and Young Edward gone from it, the castle would speedily return to its earlier state of grim fortress, stern border outpost. What then of Neddie were he to stay on, exposed to the rough harsh ways of barrack life and allowed to run wild and uncouth as any moor boy in hides and clogs?

And what of her own situation? Would a garrison prove proper habitation for a gently born maid? 'Twas not to be considered.

Master Caxton's quiet household, on the other hand, spoke for itself as a secure and fitting refuge. And for further argument in favor of a return to London there was the ripening chance that she and Neddie might well see their shattered fortunes restored, the wrongs done them rectified. Their life might even take on the brilliance, the richness that had faded so abruptly at their parents' death. Why doubt it, knowing full well that the King who was about to mount the throne claimed them as friends?

The assurance in Lord Rivers' voice, his cool confidence as he spoke of Young Edward's coming coronation day, outweighed Peg's quick fear at thought of Crook-Back, her swift revulsion against a journey to London.

Why be so foolish, she asked herself? It was Lord Rivers who had the upper hand, now.

Young Edward's guardianship was his, unchanged by any last will or testament of the dead Edward, any fickle whim of the Queen Mother, and Young Edward's affection belonged to him as well. Who, then, would stand closer to the boy king? Who other would rule the Council? Who other, in all truth, would rule the kingdom but my Lord Rivers? Hand on hilt, waiting, they may have been, he and Richard of Gloucester, as Master Pole once put it, or even at sword points, but it was Richard who must sheathe his blade and hold off for the nonce, at least.

Hesitating, turning many things over in her mind, Peg asked a question of Lord Rivers. "We will be welcome in Master Caxton's home, Neddie and I, my lord?"

"Beyond any doubt, Mistress Margaret. Have you forgot that your father not only shared most pleasant acquaintance with Master Caxton but was a generous patron to him? And with my own ears I have heard Master Caxton express keen regret at owing a debt of gratitude so long overdue in payment."

"Your words be reassuring, my lord. Send us to London when you will. I speak Neddie's gratefulness as well as my own for your concern of us."

Again Peg hesitated. "There be but one stumbling block," she admitted slowly. "Can you answer me this, my lord? Must Neddie and I eat charity at Master Caxton's and his wife's table? To do so would be to choke—to gag. We have suffered beggarhood overlong. I be sadly weary of it. Could I not be apprenticed to a task of sorts in the Caxton's household and so earn our keep? I have but little wish to live on hope of chance favors the King may toss—the dream that perchance some day—some day——"

"Nor should you, mistress. Your point be well taken." Lord Rivers considered a moment. "You stitch neatly, I have observed these past months, and you embroider with taste and skill. What better than to put your needle to use in Mistress Caxton's linen room? Further, I have marked your interest in my library, your perusal of my books. I shall bring it to Master Caxton's attention. He would profit well with a pair of young eyes at his service. For not content with the passing of ordinary hours at his press he has turned night into day with candlelight and fared the worse for it. He be half blind."

So once more Peg and Neddie stuffed their leather traveling sack with all their wordly goods. And once more, that Peg might be suitably attended, and not the sole female to be journeying in company with so many gentlemen, Susan Dow, as drip-nosed as ever, prepared to hoist her skirts well up on her skinny legs and mount her gray palfrey.

A wicker cage would perch high on the miscellany of luggage that rode with her. Young Edward had decreed that Peg should keep his thrush at Master Caxton's dwelling until he was settled in his royal quarters at the palace and had his kingly duties well in hand. "I shall be occupied from morn till night," he informed Peg grandly. "I shall be making laws. Signing documents. Advising my councilors. Telling all manner of people what I wish done. But never mind, coz. Don't worry. We shall have another one of our concerts just as soon as ever I find time for it."

On the twenty-fifth of April, St. George's Day, the King's cavalcade clattered out of the castle courtyard. Young Edward was astride a white jennet. A drift of early breeze-tossed hawthorn bloom was falling like a further trimming of ermine on his blue velvet cloak. A newly-donned cloak. That very morning, kneeling in the chapel, he had been invested with the Order of the Garter and put on its ribbon and its robes.

Neddie, riding in front of Peg's pillion, clutching the reins and insisting upon guiding their mount all by himself, had a store of eager questions to draw on as they rode along.

"Will our cousin receive his crown at once, immediately when he arrives in London?" he wanted to know.

"Within a span of weeks at lastest, I judge."

"And is his crown truly made of gold? Pure gold? Be it studded with pearls and rubies and diamonds as I have heard? And after they have given it to him in the Abbey must he wear it every day? All day? May he take it off going to bed or in his bath?"

Peg smiled. "I fancy so."

She was silent after that, and Neddie twisted round reprovingly. "Continue, Peg. Tell me more, I want to hear all about being King. Be our cousin's throne of gold, too? And must everyone from now on in all the kingdom do exactly as he wishes? Everyone? Even Lord Rivers? Even our Uncle Richard?"

"Nay. Not as yet, Neddie. Not until he has grown to be a man."

"I'd not wait if I were he. I'd make everyone mind me, beginning this very minute. 'Do this,' I'd say. 'Do that—and be quick about it!' But tell me more, Peg. When our cousin reaches London will there be a great procession?"

"Doubtless."

"Trumpets blowing? Flags flying? Bonfires? Flares set off from the river barges? 'Tis what Susan Dow declares. And we will see it! We'll see it all!"

Young Edward, as well as Neddie, was thinking about a golden crown as he rode along. Try as he would to keep his thoughts on such sad matters as a bier that he must kneel beside, a solemn farewell that must be said to the dead, his heart was leaping high within him. Was ever so bright a day? One so sweet with bud? So merry with bird song? And there would be another even more glorious, chances were, when he rode along the Strand to the Abbey for his coronation, with a thousand people cheering from the curbs and tossing their caps and bending knee to him.

With every mile that drew on to London, Young Edward knew a greater liking for his lot in life. A lift of the breeze blew the yellow hair that curled on his cloak collar and whipped the three white plumes that drooped from his jewel-brooched cap. When they brushed his cheek he laughed and tossed back his head. Soon now, in no time at all, his plumes would be set aside discarded. Prince of Wales, he? Nay. King of England, rather!

The white jennet under him was prancing in fettle as high as his own. Patting its tossing mane, Young Edward's thought turned to Gweno. One of these days he would secure for himself a dozen mounts as beautiful, as swift as his Christmas colt had been. Then, and then alone, would he be reconciled to the loss of his snatched-away Yule gift.

From Gweno it was natural to go on to thoughts of Peg. An odd maid, his coz. For all their friendship, for all the pleasure her company gave him, there was that about her that made him uneasy now and again. Those great gray eyes of hers for one thing. The manner in which they blazed whenever mention was made of His Grace, their uncle. That nameless something—why should it be fear?—that followed so closely always on their brief flaring?

Fear? For an uncle who had shown himself to be so lenient toward her? Then there was that foolish nonsense she had babbled. He had never quite forgotten it. What had their uncle named it? Phantasy? Yes. But there were moments ever so often in which he wished that the explanation might have been clearer. Curious, how this and that about it kept coming back to puzzle him. Unaccountably, Young Edward shivered in his velvet Garter mantle. He found his blithe mood dulling slightly. The April day had a sharp edge to it after all. And see? The little road puddles of spring rain water mirrored a grayness now, rather than their earlier blue. Checking his mount, he waited for Lord Rivers to ride abreast of him.

Just after sundown on the last day of their journey to London, the travelers from Ludlow Castle reined in at the hamlet of Stony-Stratford for supper and beds. Darkness was falling fast as they slid stiffly, wearily, out of their saddles in a quiet deserted inn yard and made their way to the tap-room of the Lamp and Wick.

Peg, having been bowed courteously through the door as the others stood aside for her, stepped into a low-ceilinged room that was beamed and paneled in black oak. Dimly lighted by a single pair of tallow candles, it swam in a haze of greasy odorous smoke given off from a sputtering roasting-spit that turned on the hearth. At first glance she thought the inn to be as empty as its stableyard. Dropping back her hood and unclasping her cloak, she moved to the fire, her hands spread to the welcome blaze. Then with a gasp, a little cry that could not be checked, a quick, close clutching of Neddie, she stared toward the far end of the room.

Two men in muddied leather buskins, steel-meshed tunics, had pushed back a table and were striding forward. It was Crook-Back who first dropped on one knee and offered his sword hilt to Young Edward.

"I be at your command, my liege lord."

Rising, he put an arm around Young Edward's shoulder. "I be happy to see you, nephew. His Grace, here, the Duke of Buckingham, and I have ridden fast and hard that we might be the first of your London subjects to tend our solicitude for the loss of your sire, and our felicitations upon your succession to his throne."

Chapter Eight: MOONLIGHT AND DAGGER THRUST

"... the mighty dukes, Gloucester and Buckingham."
Richard III, Act II, scene 4.

Hard and fast in all truth!

A hireling spy had reached London only the day before with belated news for Richard of Gloucester that Young Edward and his scant retinue were nearing Stony-Stratford and would sleep there on the last night of their journey to the palace.

Gloucester had galloped his horse out of London at lathering speed. A score of henchmen rode with him. All had been chosen from among his men-at-arms for a close-mouthed discretion that had been put to the test on various similar occasions.

And who more congenial a companion, his mount neck-and-neck with Gloucester's in the plume-streaming cloak-blowing race against time, than Henry Stafford, Duke of Buckingham? An opportunist, His Grace. A gentleman who had made it clear, privately, that he was willing, nay, eager, to stake the whole of his fortunes on whatever cards Gloucester chose to play.

Their early arrival at the Lamp and Wick had been a matter of mutual satisfaction. A full hour could be spent upon the final formulation of plans, the perfecting of details, and after that there would be leisure for the drinking of an unspoken toast or two and the carving of a fine, hot joint. A joint which the travelers from Ludlow Castle were cordially invited to share when they arrived at the inn.

Young Edward, pleased and flattered to have been met on his journey by such noble and powerful lords as Gloucester and Buckingham, accepted promptly. Wasting no time, he loosened his cloak, tossed aside his gauntlets and pulled up to the table by the hearth. Loading his plate from iron pots and wooden platters, he ate with gusto, tearing with his white teeth at the good juicy meat, spearing a crust of bread on his dagger-point to sop up a puddle of brown gravy, and making way with a large bowl of custard, a thick slab of fruity cake.

Neddie proved as lusty a trencherman. He stuffed until his stomach bulged under his leather jerkin, his cheeks blazing poppy-red from the raw wind of the day's ride, the heat of the hearth log, and his round eyes darting anxiously now and again toward the platters that went round for fear they might be empty before a second helping reached him.

Susan Dow, at the foot of her betters' table was equally ravenous, as were the six Ludlow henchmen. Falling upon the rougher cuts of meat served them, the basins of meal and treacle pudding passed, they washed down their supper with tankard after tankard of ale. The Duke of Gloucester

had played host for it. A brief fixing of his black eyes on
the innkeeper had fetched an almost imperceptible sly nod
of understanding in return.

Of all the company crowding the taproom, only Peg and
Master Pole, Lord Rivers and Lord Grey had little appetite.
And few words, either, to exchange among themselves or
with anyone else.

When Neddie at last pushed his plate away with a sur-
feited sigh and a yawn too wide to hide, Peg gladly excused
herself on the plea that her small brother must be put to
bed. Having made her curtseys and been supplied with a
candle, she found her way down a crooked little passageway
to a chamber furnished with a straw pallet and a chest and a
three-legged stool.

She helped Neddie with buckles and boot laces, tucked
him under a quilt, and then, undressing, blew out the
candle and lay down beside him, tense and puzzled and
filled with a foreboding that she tried to tell herself was foolish and unwarranted.

Despite her unease, weariness overtook her. She fell into
a light restless sleep with Neddie curled warm and quiet
against her. Then all at once, she was wide awake again,
sitting up, straining to listen, alert with quick alarm.

What was it she had heard—that tap-tapping? A mouse in
the wall, switching its tail? A tree bough scraping ever so
lightly against the closed window shutter?

Tap, tap. Tap, tap.

Louder now, insistent.

Tap! Tap! Tap!

On icy feet, bare against the plank floor, Peg ran to the casement. "Be someone knocking?" she whispered. "Who, pray?"

" 'Tis I, Richard Pole! Open up, mistress!"

Peg tugged at the latch and threw the shutter wide. Sir Golden Cap, a dark shape among a clump of laurel bushes, was crouching under the low sill. "Wake your brother! Snatch your cloak!" The words broke from him in a terse rush. "Out of here with all speed! We be trapped, the whole lot of us!"

Peg clutched the sill. "My uncle's doing?"

"Aye, but no time for words, mistress. There ben't a minute to lose."

Peg stumbled through the darkness to the wall hooks where her clothes hung. Fumbling with buttons and clasps and lacings, she fastened skirts and bodice, gartered her stockings, and stepped into her slippers. Then she leaned over the pallet and shook Neddie. "Wake! Wake," she whispered frantically. "Wake!"

With a hand clapped over his mouth she silenced his sleep-dazed protests. "Your boots, your breeches. Don them, little brother. Now, your jerkin next. Here be the holes for your arms."

She dragged him to the window. "Out with you! You see Master Pole waiting to catch you?"

When Neddie was shoved over the sill, Peg followed, bunching her petticoats, catching up her cloak.

The window was low, and a full moon lighted the drop to the ground. But though it helped her to a sure footing, the white, cold radiance was a pitiless foe as she and Richard Pole, dragging Neddie between them, scuttled for cover.

The inn yard they skirted was as unconcealing as a small square lidless box.

Where to hide? Where, oh where?

Peg framed a wordless prayer, and then a second later Richard Pole was making for a shallow refuse ditch that ran alongside the Lamp and Wick. In a splash of foul-smelling water, a splatter of mud, they crossed to its far bank and dropped down, huddling and breathless, in a tangle of reeds and willows.

Somewhere a dog barked, and their hearts hammered loud in their ears. When an owl flew out of its nest hooting and flapping its wings, Peg cowered lower, and with a small agonized moan, shut her eyes tightly. When she dared to open them again it was to peer fearfully across the ditch to the inn.

She pulled at Richard Pole's sleeve. "What happened? What's wrong? Tell me! Tell me! And where be my cousin? Lord Rivers? Lord Grey?"

Her voice was shaking, her thin body shivering.

"Steady, mistress." Sir Golden Cap put an arm around her. She could feel its comforting strength and warmth through her wet, ditch-bedraggled cloak. "You shall hear all in good time, but ask me nothing now." He shot a glance toward the Lamp and Wick, listened sharply for a moment and then stood up, one hand out to steady Neddie to his feet, the other to Peg. "Let's be off! You hear the stir in the inn yard? You see the glimmer of torchlight? They've found us gone. Crook-Back's men be scattering for a search I doubt not. There'll be a hue and cry raised hereabouts."

"But where to flee, Master Pole? Where find a hiding place?"

"What matter for the moment? Any other place at all will prove a safer burrow than this. Come!"

Sir Golden Cap plunged through the willow thickets. Peg scrambled after him, dragging Neddie the while she begged him to cease his sleepy protests, his loud indignant questioning.

Where were they going, he wanted to know as they stumbled through the dark? Why had Peg pulled him out of his warm covers at the inn? Why had she and Master Pole made him splash through so wet, so stinking a ditch? Did they know how cold he was? And why must they hurry so, why crouch so low, as they made their way through the owl-haunted night?

"Hush, hush, little brother! A soft voice if you please. There be no need to cry out—the owls will do you no harm. And would you wake all the other birds who sleep in their nests by so noisy a progress? Nay. Surely not."

"But why are we here in these black lonely woods? Answer me, Peg. And where be our cousin and everyone else?"

"Young Edward snores in his bed, chances are," Richard Pole broke in quickly, reassuringly, as he halted for a moment that Peg and Neddie might again catch their breath. "And a good joke should we arrive in London ahead of him, wouldn't you say? A proper lazybones, the Prince. You'd not catch me asleep with town so close, nor you either, I'll wager. So here we go, on our way again, Neddie. See if you can catch me. I shall be a hare and you shall be a hound."

Once more Sir Golden Cap darted ahead with Peg and Neddie trying their hardest to keep up to him. Scurrying from larch copse to clustered beechwood trunks, wading knee-deep through a brook, wriggling under a hedge, clambering over stone walls, they traversed woods and meadowland and ploughed fields. All of it was a huge jest now to Neddie. Panting though he was and aching-legged, he kept on without complaint. And a sluggard, truly, his royal cousin, content to lie in bed with trumpet blare so near, waving pennons all but in sight.

Just at dawn they came to the fringe of an early-blossoming cherry orchard. Beyond it was a farm cottage with breakfast smoke rising from a hole in its thatched roof. While Peg and Neddie sank down exhausted on the dew-soaked ground, Richard Pole strode off to knock at the cottage door and exchange a penny for a loaf of black bread.

Having learned by cautious inquiry that they were well off the London highway and had left Stony-Stratford a good distance behind, he came back declaring that they must eat and rest before continuing their journey.

Neddie was asleep after his first bite, his curly head sag-

ging against Peg's breast and then it was that Sir Golden
Cap gave her an account of the night's happening. "My tale
ben't a pleasant one," he warned her soberly. "Best take a
hold on yourself, mistress." Then he began his story by going back to the Lamp and Wick taproom after Peg had left it
for her bedchamber.

The henchmen from Ludlow had taken an early and be-
fuddled departure for the stable. Their tankards had
banged down on the table at a sharp word from Lord Rivers.
Susan Dow climbed to a pallet in the inn's garret. Young
Edward had departed for bed shortly after ten o'clock struck,
reluctant for all his yawns to leave the card game that he
and Richard Pole had been playing.

Neither Lord Rivers, nor Lord Grey, the Duke of Buckingham nor the Duke of Gloucester showed any intention
of seeking their chambers. Two chessboards had been set up
and they were playing wordlessly.

Richard Pole, admitting to himself a growing though
vague unease, a restlessness, and knowing that sleep would
be hard come by, had taken himself to the stable. His
mount had been fretted on the day's journey by a saddle gall.
As good a time then as any to salve it.

The cobbled yard, washed in moonlight, was quiet when
he crossed it except for an inquiring whinny or two, a
momentary moving about among the Ludlow horses that
were tied to rings along the brick wall.

Once inside the stable he had stepped over his sprawled-
out heavily-breathing traveling companions from the castle

and made for the harness-room, hoping to lay hands upon a jar of ointment.

He found one readily, thanks to the moonlight, and in another moment would have gone outside to his horse when he heard the ceiling boards creak overhead.

His first casual upward glance turned to a stare.

Another board had creaked and at the far end of the stable a trap door was slowly stealthily opening. A pair of legs dropped over the edge of the opening and found footing on the rungs of a tall ladder. The man who was starting to climb down from the hayloft wore the flash of a naked dagger at his belt. Crowding him was the dangle of another pair of legs.

In the brief second granted him by that back-turned unseeing descent, Richard Pole had slipped behind the harness-room door. Flattening himself, his body as rigid as wood, he had watched six men in all swarm down the ladder. The moonlight that glinted on their dagger blades shone as brightly on the silver shoulder badges that marked them hirelings of the Boar.

They had gone about their business quickly. There had been no more to it than the muffling of a groggy outcry or two, and the swift sure thrust of those glinting blades.

"And when 'twas over? What then, Master Pole?" Peg whispered the question from the depths of a wretched queasiness that had rushed upon her.

The blood—the blood—— The soaking red pools of it on the stable's plank floor. The dead men littering the floor,

arms and legs flung out, sprawled all which way, so dread-
fully still. Her stomach heaved. Sweat dampened the roots
of her hair. Her palms were clammy.

"When 'twas over? You go too fast, mistress. There be
more to tell."

Grimly, Master Pole continued his chronicle. "Mind you,
the inn yard was light as day under the moon. And while I
watched, cursing myself for a helpless dolt, my hands tied
against so many, I saw the taproom door open and yet another knot of Boar's men come out, dragging what at first
sight I took to be two sacks. But nay. 'Twas my lord Rivers
and my lord Grey, God help them. Trussed like fowl for a
hearth-spit, they were, and gagged with a gauntlet, from the
look of it, stuffed in each of their mouths. By Heaven, a
sorry sight! And there I was, hiding behind a door—skulking
—playing the part of a weak-gutted craven——"

Sir Golden Cap broke off abruptly. When he could go
on, every word came reluctantly and heavy with shame.
"There was nothing for it but to watch. Nothing for it but
to see them flung across saddle pommels, then, and carried
off to Castle Pontefract."

"Pontefract?"

"A holding of your uncle's, I take it, mistress, and one
that lies somewhere close to Stony-Stratford, from what my
ears picked up. Not that I lingered long, pricking them. Far
from it. 'Twas out of the harness-room window with me the
moment I dared make a move. And then to your shutter as
quick as ever I could get there."

"But what of Young Edward? Oh, to think I ran—to think I paid him no heed—— A most base desertion of him, yours and mine, Master Pole."

"Spare yourself, Mistress Margaret. Self-berating mends nothing. Our leaving of Young Edward is over with—a thing that lies behind us. And I be more than a little sorry that you think ill of me for my share in what we have done. Believe me, I called upon all my judgement in weighing what course to take. Brief, in all truth, the time alloted me for decision. And best by far, it struck me as I climbed out of that window, to offer what succor I could to you and to Neddie and to forget Young Edward. 'Let him sleep,' I told myself. 'He be safe enough for the nonce.' "

"Safe?" Peg cried it out incredulously. "Safe, left to my uncle's mercy? By what reasoning, Master Pole?"

"By my faith in Crook-Back's slyness, mistress. Who be more of a master hand at deception than he? And what craftier trick could he play than to ride into London side-by-side with Young Edward for all the town to mark? A favorite uncle. A favorite nephew. You see his design, Mistress Margaret? And a pretty pattern to it, with youthful King and kindly protector so openly, so affectionately close. Aye! And time a-plenty later for another murder. Let suspicions be lulled, first. Let there be a minimum of awkward questions and undue prying."

"But will no one guess the truth? Will no one inquire concerning Lord Rivers' and Lord Grey's absence when Young Edward reaches London? Will no one suspect foul play? Will the Queen herself not call my uncle to account, with Lord Grey so well-loved a son, Sir Anthony so prime a favorite?"

"I yet say my faith lies in Crook-Back. I'd trust him any day for the cooking up of lies. 'Twill be easy enough for him to fob off the Queen, so full of tears now, so distraught with her widowhood. Let her ply him with a hundred questions, and he'll find a hundred answers, each more plausible than the last."

"But Young Edward, what of him? He'll not suspect? You think he'll have no inkling of treachery when he wakes upon the morrow?"

"None. As I see it, he'll swallow Crook-Back's lies as though they were honey cakes, and ask for more. What be he when all is said and done but a simple gullible babe, scarce out of swaddling clothes?"

"A babe? He be as old as I, Master Pole."

"In years, I grant you, but a mewling infant none the less. Remember, mistress, yours was a harder teething-ring than any he knew, and it makes a difference, that."

Peg had no argument to offer. Her arms tightened around the sleeping Neddie. "It was my uncle's plan to put my brother and me out of the way as he did those others?" she asked after a moment's silence. "Let me hear the truth— that was why you came to my window, Master Pole?"

"Yes, for I had no wish to gamble upon Gloucester's moves, mistress. Who was I, to guess his next play? And what more convenient place than the Lamp and Wick had he seen fit to silence you? A murder more, a murder less, would matter little to his minions were their palms greased richly enough."

Again Peg's arms tightened around Neddie. Master Pole glanced remorsefully at her white face. "Questions—questions—I have let you ask too many of them, mistress. And I have wearied you, answering them at such length and in so grisly a manner. My tongue has run away with me. Why not lie down and seek sleep as Neddie has done? I too, shall stretch out."

"But when we have rested, what then?"

"Why not set our feet toward London and the Red Pale? I can think of no safer lodging for you and Neddie than with Master Caxton, nor any wiser course than the carrying out of Lord Rivers' arrangements for you."

"And you, Master Pole? You also will remain in London?"

"Nay. I must hie me back to Ludlow with word to Sir John of this night's foul work. After that—who knows? But close your eyes now, mistress. Shall we let the morrow take heed for itself?"

With a faint tired smile, a murmured good-night, Peg followed Sir Golden Cap's advice. Her arms around Neddie, she fell asleep.

A dawn wind sprang up, sending a rain of fluttering cherry petals down upon her. Turning, in the midst of some troubled dream or other, she sighed, and drew her cloak closer.

Richard Pole, his head pillowed on his arms, glanced toward her.

A pity that Mistress Margaret had no warmer blanket than those drifting sweet-scented petals. And the blame his in part that her slumber was so uneasy. How pale her face in the dawn light. How dark the circles beneath her eyes where the half moons of her tawny lashes lay. And was ever in all the world a maid so put-upon, or sorrier-fated?

Peg stirred again.

This time, before he himself fell asleep, Sir Golden Cap moved nearer, and spreading out his own cloak, shared it with her.

Chapter Nine: A BOY WHO WAS KING

"Welcome, sweet Prince, to London———"
Richard III, Act II, SCENE 1.

At the Lamp and Wick, Young Edward woke to a hand on his shoulder and a brusque shaking. Richard of Gloucester plucked away his quilts. "Up with you, nephew, and lose no time. You think this be a morning to lie abed with all of London waiting to set eyes upon their King?"

"I shall garb myself swift as lightning, uncle." Yawning and stretching, Young Edward blinked round him at the unfamiliar room and then leapt out of bed and reached hurriedly for his breeches and tunic. Richard turned to the door. "You slept well, I trust?" he inquired at the threshold. "Passed the night without disturbance? A boisterous lot, your men-at-arms, and a trifle in their cups. The stableyard was not as quiet as it might have been, methought."

"I heard naught, uncle." Young Edward yawned again. "A good thing you called me, else I should even yet be asleep."

When he was booted and cloaked and capped, he hurried down to the taproom, and finding himself the sole person at table, fell quickly upon the ham and porridge and bread that were set out. Not half a jest that the King himself was the last one down to breakfast on so important a day!

When he heard the jingle and clink of bit and bridle, a clatter of hooves and a readying for departure in the stable yard, he dropped spoon and knife and rushed outside.

The Boar's henchmen had already mounted. Gloucester and Buckingham were ready to throw leg over saddle. Young Edward's surprised glance swept the stableyard. "Where be my Ludlow men, uncle? I see none of them. Nor do I see Lord Rivers or Lord Grey. And where be my friend Richard Pole? Where be my cousins? They have overslept, the lot of them? Why were they not roused, pray? And must we waste the morning dallying till they breakfast and mount?"

"We wait for no one." The Duke of Gloucester settled himself in the saddle and picked up his reins. "Mount, nephew. It so happened that Lord Rivers and I clashed in argument last night after you had sought your bed. We both have chosen to take separate ways for the nonce. And having keen wish for the pleasure of your company I bargained that you should ride under my standard rather than his for the remainder of the journey."

"You compliment me, uncle. But why the clash you speak of, the argument? 'Twas no serious falling out, I hope."

"A difference of opinions, let us say. A taking of sides— opposite sides—concerning your future. All at once, Lord Rivers finds you over-young for the throne. As green as a new apple he puts it. And accordingly harbors a wish to postpone your rule until such birthday be reached that he considers suitable."

"And to add to the nonsense, your guardian would keep you tied fast to lessons, Your Highness," the Duke of Buckingham broke in with a little laugh. "Would hold you a schoolboy from now until Doomsday. You approve the notion?"

"A schoolboy?" Astounded, aghast, Young Edward stared from Buckingham to Gloucester. "Lord Rivers would thrust me back to so stupid a level? Would bind me to books again?"

"Exactly so, nephew. Further study would be to your great benefit, he claims, and would serve you well once you be grown. But a zealot to my mind, Lord Rivers, and over-conscientious in his role of tutor. Though in all fairness, I perchance should condone the fault. Natural enough that so brilliant a man of letters should yearn to make a scholar of you."

"But he shan't. He shan't." Young Edward's protest was vehement, indignant. "You told him off last night, uncle? You spoke out for me? Then my thanks to you a thousand times over. And to you, as well, Lord Henry, if you shared in taking my part."

Despite his gratitude, his relief, there was a shade of concern on Young Edward's face. "Where be Lord Rivers at the moment, uncle?" he asked. "Not ridden back to Ludlow in a huff, I trust? Strange that he has not yet greeted me this morning. Mind you, he has been a most kind and good

friend to me always, and a friend whom I would not wish
to lose, for all his narrow-minded and over-zealous ways concerning my welfare."

"You shall see him soon," Richard of Gloucester promised smoothly. "And doubtless there will be amicable agree-
ment among us all in due course. But at the moment he be
ahead of us, already London bound, and your Ludlow escort with him."

"Does he think to put this talk of books before my
mother?"

"More than that. 'Twould not surprise me should he have
wish to search out certain like-minded councilors."

" 'Like-minded?' There be other nobles who find me too
few in years to sit the throne?"

"The truth in a nutshell, nephew."

Young Edward flushed. "So. They think me a child, do
they? Only wait! They shall see! Yes. And change their tune
if they know what's good for them." Defiantly, his head
held high, he asked, "What care I for Lord Rivers and his
ilk? Let them set themselves against me or not. A king has
friends aplenty. Small loss, to drop the false ones."

Richard of Gloucester's eyes were fathomless. The Duke
of Buckingham noncommital. With their horses reined out
of the stableyard and on to the highway, the Boar's company
rode toward London.

Scorching resentment blackened the first long miles for
Young Edward. A plague upon my Lord Rivers! Maledic-
tions upon his head for his impertinent, silly interference.

And as for Richard Pole and his cousin Peg riding off without him, that too was a galling grievance. Might they not have managed a good-bye? At very least, one single hasty word of farewell, no matter how early a start they had made? Their surprising departure hurt and baffled Young Edward more than he chose to admit.

But why let thought of them spoil his day, he argued with himself? There were plenty of other things to dwell on, were there not? And oh, how bright, how promising a morning. No one, no one in the world could cheat him of the glory lying ahead in London. More like than not, cheering mobs were even now swarming the curbs. More like than not, the river was already clotted with loaded barges sunk to the water line by hundreds and hundreds of his cap-waving subjects.

Fancy the shouts, the clamor of bells when he rode into the city! He would sit tall and straight in his saddle. He would make himself look every inch a king. Would his father know, perchance? Would his father be proud of him? Young Edward hoped it with all his heart.

As he rode along he admitted on second thought that he could well afford to forgive Master Pole and Mistress Peg for their desertion of him on so great a day. Master Pole, after all, was tied by the bonds of his squireship to ride wherever Lord Rivers rode. And what other course for Peg to follow, either? She was naught but a beggar maid. She must go where she was bid.

Quite a different story for someone as fortunate as himself! The King of England could do exactly as he pleased. Yes. On his Coronation Day he would present his uncle of Gloucester with a very special present. Something truly handsome. The Duke of Buckingham should have a gift as well. And so should everyone else who upheld him against any further foolish notions on Lord Rivers' part. But why think on his tutor now, with London drawing so close?

London! London! A few more miles and he would come upon the palace, all its banners aflaunt in his honor. He would ride past the Abbey where his throne waited.

Looking down the river, he would see the Tower looming against the blue bright sky. The Tower, custodian of the Crown, the Ball and the Sceptre that would make him truly king. The Tower, built by Julius Caesar, men said. Ancient. Walled. Impregnable. Oh, London! London!

It was late afternoon when the Boar's cavalcade rode into the city by way of Bishop's Gate. At Hornsea Park they were met by the Lord Mayor and a company of aldermen and sheriffs, all in scarlet, and by a throng of commoners dressed in violet.

There was general approval from the crowds as they craned and commented upon the somber black velvet habit and cloak that Richard of Gloucester wore, and upon his grave mien.

Proper enough that His Grace should mourn a dead brother so respectfully and with such open grief. But on the other hand, London had been steeped too deep in gloom of late. Time now for a change. Enough of the funereal.

The King was dead. Long live the King!

And so uproariously, they gave cheer upon cheer for Young Edward, decked out in the ermined Garter cloak that was so royal and so splendid for all its travel stains.

Huzza! Huzza! Huzza! There were cheers for Young Edward's three white plumes. Cheers for his gilt spurs. Cheers for his snowy jennet, caparisoned with crimson and cloth-of-gold. Cheers for his blue eyes and for the set of his yellow head.

The shouting and the fanfare of trumpets followed him to St. Paul's churchyard where he dismounted, and in company with the Bishop of London who had ridden to the city gate to meet him, went inside the cathedral to bend knee at the jeweled golden shrine of St. Erkenwald. It was what every king did. And in no way did he wish to differ from all those who had gone before him.

When his praying was done, Richard of Gloucester announced to him that he was to spend the night at the Bishop's Palace close by.

"The Bishop's Palace, rather than my own? But why not ride on to Westminster, uncle? I had looked forward to it. And what of my lady mother waiting me? Surely I should seek her out without further delay?"

"Time enough on the morrow, nephew. Courtesy demands that we accept tonight's hospitality with good grace."

The subject was closed.

Later, at supper time, when Young Edward came down a

stone stair to join Gloucester and Buckingham and his host, he found a company of guests gathered to break bread in his honor.

The group was a small one and select. My lords Thomas and William Stanley. Lord Hastings. Francis, Viscount Lovel. John Morton, Bishop of Ely. Sir Richard Ratcliff. Sir Thomas Vaughn. Sir Richard Catesby. Councilors, all, Young Edward wondered? And who among them were on Lord Rivers' side, who on his? There was no telling. All present showed him every respect, every kindness.

When the table was spread, they laid choice tid-bits off their own plates onto his. He was plied with the largest oysters, the most quivering jellies, the plumpest of sea bird breasts, plover eggs caudled in butter. When a loving cup went round he quaffed from it not once but twice, being determined to prove himself a man in their eyes.

A moment came, however, when he fought mightily to keep his eyes open, heavy as they were with travel-weariness and the stupor that his gluttony had brought upon him. And all the length of the table his courtiers were smiling indulgently and bidding him seek his bed. He must be wide awake, bright-eyed on the morrow for a host of processions and masques and water pageants that would fete him.

"And I shall be, my lords, believe me."

Young Edward spoke up eagerly, only to add with quick sobering and a guilty pang, "But first off, come morning, I must go to my mother. I be grievously tardy even now in paying my devotion. My father's tomb calls me as well, for a prayer and—and for a leave-taking."

"Admirable sentiments, nephew, most admirable. But for all that, I fear me that a visit to Westminster Palace must wait."

Richard of Gloucester dipped fastidious hands into a basin of warm perfumed water as he spoke and dried them on a linen towel. "I have heard tell since our arrival here in London that your Queen mother craves nothing so much as to be left solitary with her grief. Unfortunate lady, 'tis known to me that she passes day and night in the dark crypt where your sire lies and refuses to be comforted, drowning herself in tears the while."

"All the more reason then that I hasten to her, uncle."

"Nay. You fail of understanding. She can abide no one with her—no one. Has banished your brother and sisters as well as any others from her company. According to report, little Dickon too mopes most dolefully. Why not, with the palace so unwholesome a dwelling at the moment for one so young as he? A morbidness to it. A melancholy. 'Twould be wise, methinks, if both you and he took residence in the Tower until this dismal mourning season be passed, and until your crown be donned."

"The Tower?" Young Edward's face clouded. "Why the Tower? Have you forgot that Westminster Palace be home to Dickon and to me? Home, second that is, to Ludlow. However should we pass the days without our bowling green, our tilt yard, our stables? You'd have us waste the summer time, uncle? Have you forgot my liking for song? Think on the Abbey so near at hand with its chorals, its choir master."

"His Majesty puts the case well, Your Grace."

It was Lord Hastings who tossed the casual words, looking up from the cracking of a walnut, and Young Edward turned to him gratefully. "I thank you, my lord! You heard, uncle?"

John Morton, Bishop of Ely, was the next to champion him. Toying with his goblet, his eyes on the red brimming wine, he stated slowly, "The palace be my choice as well, Your Grace. Its gloom will pass in due course. And what be Dickon's moping but a natural grief? 'Twill heal itself soon enough, and all the quicker when his brother joins him."

" 'Tis true, uncle. I shall cheer Dickon in the very wink of an eye. Oh, the palace for us by all means! 'Tis twice the better choice for our dwelling than the Tower."

"Enough, nephew. And may I ask no further discussion from you, as well, my lords? Not that your opinions lack value——"

"But, uncle——"

"Enough, I say, nephew. Westminster must wait. It is too late an hour by far for further discussion. Off to bed with you."

Richard of Gloucester put it clearly, coldly. Young Edward stared. Had his uncle given an order?

There was little doubt of it. Crimson faced, humiliated, Young Edward stood stiffly while one by one the nobles round the table rose to bid him a grave courteous good-night. Inwardly raging, biting down hard upon the words ready to his tongue, he turned away abruptly and marched out of the banquet hall with his head high.

Question after question pricked sharp as thorns as he climbed the stairs to his bedchamber. An order! A terse sharp command! How had his uncle dared? Now, after all, did his own preference truly lie with His Grace of Gloucester over Lord Rivers? To be honest, did either one uncle or the other please him in slightest degree at the moment? Nay. Both of them had overstepped their bounds. Where was their due respect, their concern for the wishes of a boy who was king? Flown out the window, 'twould seem!

Young Edward rubbed his head fretfully. Enough to lay him low, its swirl and ache. No pleasure, either, the heaving of his stomach. Wiser perchance had he let that second helping of goose liver pass him by and that second helping of chestnut stuffing served up with the roasted swan. And far, far better had he said nay to the refilling of his wine cup.

When he reached his bedchamber, Young Edward was sick in a silver basin. Afterwards, spent and subdued, he climbed weakly into a velvet-canopied bed.

Lying there, close to the edge of sleep, he remembered something that Peg had declared once upon a time at Ludlow Castle. He had been angered by it. But now he knew that it was true.

Their Uncle of Gloucester's eyes were indeed a toad's. Black. Jewel-bright. Unwinking. Cold.

"Aye, me, I see the downfall of our house!
The tiger now hath seized the gentle hind."
Richard III, Act II, SCENE 4.

"Boy! Boy! You there with the broom. Lend me an ear. Be I nearing the house of Master William Caxton?"

Susan Dow put the question from the back of the palfrey that had carried her from Stony-Stratford into London and through a maze of crowded evil-smelling streets and lanes to the pleasanter greener part of town that was known as the City of Westminster.

The apprentice boy who was sweeping the curb in front of a baker's shop nodded, with a curious eye for the bird cage slung across her saddle. "You be close to it as bread and butter, old dame. Follow your nose past the Abbey. Turn west at the end o' it for St. Anne's Chapel and the Almons- rye, and then you'll come on a timbered dwelling with Master Caxton's red shield hung on its front. You can't miss. You'll know you be there by the thump of his press. A din to be heard from dawn to dark. And a bit louder than strikes some folk's fancy, if truth be told."

He gave another glance at the cage and grinned. "I be

sorry for your warbler. 'Twill need a sound-box tough as leather bellows to chirp above the racket at Master Caxton's house."

He turned to his sweeping, and a few minutes later Susan Dow had arrived at the Sign of the Red Pale. Searching out Master Caxton's scullery door, she knocked, and then being directed up a wooden stair, found her way to Peg's little, dark-wainscoted room at the top of the house where a slice of window looked out through green beech trees to the Abbey spires and to the busy, barge-crowded Thames.

Susan Dow closed the door behind her with a bang, thumped her wicker cage down on a stool and faced Peg irately. "A pretty trick, your giving me the slip from the Lamp and Wick," she scolded with a waggle of a bony finger in Peg's face. "A fine diddling of poor old Susan Dow, left behind to fret and stew and make her way into town as best she could. Only lend me a hairbrush, mistress, and I'll take it to your bottom gladly."

"Nay. Forgive me, good dame. I be truly sorry if I caused you concern. A difficult matter to explain, I grant you, but there was no help for it—the whole of it out of my hands—and nothing for it but to run, believe me. To take my leave, that is——" Hurriedly Peg amended her words as best she could, but she was too late. Susan Dow's little peering curiosity-ridden eyes were fixed on her bright as beads.

"You ran, did you, mistress? Took to your heels? Humph! And what about Young Edward riding into London with His Grace of Gloucester rather than with my Lord Rivers? Something's up, eh? What gives, my pretty pippin? Do I smell a rat?"

"A rat?" Peg fingered the latch of the cage door, her eyes dropping under Susan Dow's prying. "I—I don't know what you mean. And tell me something of your own journey, beldame. You rode here alone from Stony-Stratford?"

"How else, with the Lamp and Wick as empty of escort as a sieve be of water? What's more, not so much as a single hostler in sight to fetch my palfrey. Strange, the inn to lack a groom. Or had its stableman been sent packing for a good reason, think you?"

"Knowing naught of how the Lamp and Wick be staffed I can scarce make answer." Again Peg avoided Susan Dow's bright eyes. "But doubtless you put question to the innkeeper regarding our—our absence, our sudden departure? Then what, pray, did he have to say, gammer?"

"You'd like to know, would you? You be wondering what manner of lies he spoke with his ugly slit of a fish mouth? He gave out little, the old cod. No more than that Lord Rivers and His Grace had taken it into their high-and-mighty heads to hurry the lot of you off to London before ever the sun was up. But in a pig's eye, that one, mistress! You think I believed him? For if Lord Rivers had equal voice in the matter why so early a stir with naught told us the night before when you and Master Neddie and I took to our beds? And why, with everyone else knocked up, would he leave me snoring and thus do you out of a serving woman the remainder of the way to London?"

Susan Dow sniffed vigorously and then pinched her long nose between thumb and forefinger. "A rat somewhere for certain, ducky. Phew! And a high ripe stench to it that will take more than one pommander ball to sweeten. So why not loose your tongue? Let's hear what went on while I was a-bed. Spew it out, ducks! There's a good juicy tale to be told, am I right?"

"A tale, truly," Peg barely whispered.

"But a button on your lips, eh? And who stitched it there, that be my next question. You'll speak out, or shall I make a guess?"

"Nay, have done! Say no more, ask me nothing."

"Ah, now, my pretty, why so frightened? You be blanched as any almond! 'Tis only old Susan Dow who makes query of you, and where the harm in that? I'll button my own mouth tight as you like, if it please you. Aye, and drop my questions to the bottom of a well rather than set you all a-shake. Though mind, I've got eyes in my head as well as the next one."

Susan Dow gave a ghoulish cackle. "A lax fellow with a mop, my friend Fish Mouth. What say when I tell you that those ruddy blotches on his stable floor were plain to see as my own thumb when I took myself round to saddle up."

"Blotches?" Peg put the question faintly, white to her lips.

"Aye. Blotches. You've seen a butcher's apron, ducky?"

Susan Dow cackled again with a grisly relish as she settled her puce-colored cloak round her shoulders and tightened the strings of its hood. "I be off for the palace to pick up my broom in the royal nursery," she announced, "but you shall see me back for another cozy chat one of these days. Meanwhile, mind you keep an eye on Master Chirp here. He and I be thick as thieves—ben't us, birdie, after our jaunt from Stony-Stratford with none but each other for company? And remember, ducky, 'tis as I said—there be a button on my lips when it comes to the Lamp and Wick. The gentry's quarrels be their own. What business of mine to prattle, so long as Young Edward be out of it with a safe skin?"

Susan Dow was gone then, skipping down the stairs on her nimble skinny old legs, and Peg heard a clop-clop-clop as her palfrey plodded away from the Red Pale.

How much of the truth had she guessed? And was her promise of a guarded tongue to be trusted?

Young Edward's thrush began to twitter as though trying to reassure Peg with a Yes! Yes! Yes! Grateful to it, she opened its cage and let it hop into the cup of her hand.

"I be happy to see you again, little bird," she confided. "And I trust you'll sing as cheeringly for me here in London as you did at Ludlow. My spirits are at low ebb, I be sorry to relate—for though this be a most pleasant house as you will find, shall I ever forget the horrid road that led us here?"

Peg shivered as she stroked the thrush and held it close to her cheek, and then resolutely she thrust thought of the Lamp and Wick behind her. Up here in this high snug little room with the rustle of beech leaves outside her window and the Abbey spires pushing up to Heaven, she had far better things to think about. Master Caxton and Mistress Maude, to begin with—kind, kind Master Caxton, kind Mistress Maude, with a heart as large and warm as her motherly bosom.

Could any welcome have been truer, or spoken with more sincerity than theirs when she and Master Pole, dragging a weary whimpering Neddie between them, had crept to the door of the Red Pale to make themselves known and to pour out their chronicle of Crook-Back's treachery? Nay. No one's. And though they had arrived but two nights past, she and Neddie had already found a foster home.

Master Caxton and Mistress Maude had declared it so from the first moment. Putting aside their own shocked dismay, their fear of the probable fate in store for such close and cherished friends as Lord Rivers and Lord Grey, they had offered her a roof for as long as she and Neddie stood in need of one, and they had urged shelter on Master Pole for whatever sojourn he might make in London.

While their story was in the telling, Mistress Maude had ordered a supper laid and the brewing of a hot posset, that a tinge of color might be brought back to Peg's face.

Afterwards, she had pulled Neddie onto her ample lap, not minding in the least the rumpling of its fine silk. "Will you be my boy?" she had asked him. "I be sadly in need of one, so say you will; there's a lamb pie." And then she had given him a hug, laughing when he wriggled away and popping a honey-ball into his mouth for him to suck upon.

That had not been all. She had turned Peg's bedcovers

down with her own hands, and when Peg was lying under the quilt, she had leaned over and kissed the top of her red-brown curls. "Good night, my child," she had said. "Sleep well. And God keep you."

The next morning when Sir Golden Cap had told his hosts that he must depart at once for Ludlow, Master Caxton had insisted upon making him the present of a mount to re-place the steed that had been left behind in the stableyard at Stony-Stratford. Promptly, a servant had been dispatched to a nearby mews for its purchase.

" 'Twill be no easy wrench, my leaving," Sir Golden Cap had confessed to Master Caxton and Mistress Maude as they sat at breakfast. "A hard choice verily betwixt Young Edward here in town and Sir John at Ludlow. Would I might cut myself in two and serve them both. A low das-tardly act, to most eyes I fear me, my riding off now with His Highness left behind in so risky a spot."

"Look upon it more reasonably, young sir. No need to lash yourself with so harsh a whip. Who could judge you wrongly?" Master Caxton, peeling an apple and dipping each neat quarter into a salt-cellar, had done his best to hearten Sir Golden Cap. " 'Tis only fitting that you seek your knight's banner. What more proper course? There be no question of it. A matter of duty, that you hie yourself to Sir John quick as beast can carry you, as anyone of sound judgement would agree."

"So I tell myself, Master Caxton, but a hollow ring to it, a lack of conviction to my ears all the same. There be few enough in town who'll stand fast to Young Edward in time of need. How many would cling to him, think you, should Gloucester press in closer?"

"You ask a difficult question, my friend. My answer can only be surmise." Master Caxton reached for another apple. "First off, though, there be a hundred, perchance a thousand, nobles who gag on Gloucester's very name. I can count you half, at very least, among them, who admit outright that they've no slightest wish to see Young Edward on the throne. His tender years speak against him with some. His Yorkish heritage with others. The time be arrived for a Lancastrian to swing into the saddle, so the majority say. And give them a man, no mere boy."

A spiral of thin russet parings uncurled on Master Caxton's plate as his knife went round and round the polished firm-fleshed apple that had been carried over in Mistress Maude's storeroom since harvest-time the autumn before. "Let me point you out my lords Courtney and Pembroke and Oxford for example," he continued, munching reflectively. "Methinks I can state fairly that they mirror the opinion of many. And while it be true enough that they have no stomach for open murder and choose to wear a pious blindfold at the moment, they'll be the first, you may be certain, to cry a secret chorus of thanks should Richard do away with our unfortunate sorry-circumstanced King."

"They'll back the Tudor, will they? Turn a cold shoulder to Young Edward? Leave him with fewer than a dozen knights to fight his cause, and those loyal from naught but pity? I take it then that you see the picture in like manner as Sir John, Master Caxton. A gloomy view! Be it any wonder that I feel a churl, deserting His Highness when he be so hard pressed for friends?"

"A matter of duty, let me say again Master Pole. Simple, clear duty."

"Would I could believe it. But no more of my doubts, my regrets. On with the latest London talk, I pray you, that I may carry it back to Ludlow. And answer me this first, Master Caxton. Who will join forces with Crook-Back, think you, should swords be drawn and open combat declared?"

"Such leeches as Catesby and Ratcliff it goes without saying. Yes, and Lord Lovel as well, along with all too great a number of henchmen and yeomen who wear his silver dog on their sleeve."

"And what be the news concerning Lord Hastings' loyalty? What of the Stanleys' frame of mind?"

" 'Tis too early in the day to state with conviction, Master Pole. But carry word to Sir John that Hastings wavers, so the whisper goes, and that the Stanleys, both William and Thomas, be reputed to be playing a game within a game. I doubt me that Richard himself knows with any sound assurance where their allegiance will light. And upon my life, what a bagful of gold he'd give, were a bond sealed between himself and them! And half of the kingdom in the bargain, I trow, if he had it to offer—which Heaven forbid he ever shall!"

Like a pendulum, talk had swung back and forth then

between Master Caxton and Master Pole as to this noble who assuredly would pledge sword to the Tudor, or to that one who, for the currying of future favors, would stand firm for Richard.

Peg, remembering it, sighed as she stroked Young Edward's thrush, her eyes dreaming. A long, weary wait 'twould be before she could hope to hear Master Pole's voice again. And a long way off, Ludlow. League upon league.

That very morning, although already it seemed an age ago, Sir Golden Cap had bade farewell to Mistress Maude and Master Caxton. Peg and Neddie had followed him out of the door to the curb and watched him mount his new bay steed. A faint pink crept into Peg's cheeks as she thought upon the manner in which Sir Golden Cap had looked down on her from the saddle.

"Be your eyes a true gray, Mistress Margaret?" he had asked surprisingly. "Or rather ben't there a peaty hue to them? Something of that same brownish green that glen water knows when bracken shades its pools? 'Twould appear so, now and again."

Before she could find an answer, he had ridden away, but at the turn of the lane just beyond St. Anne's, he had looked back and waved. Then the flutter of her own kerchief had followed him out of sight.

The days that followed Master Pole's going proved much of a kind. Mistress Maude, at Peg's earnest plea, set her to the hemming and embroidery of household linens and began her instruction in the art of making simples, while Master Caxton, blinking out of watery, blurred eyes, had implored her help in the sorting and indexing of a pile of manuscripts.

The month of May passed.

All of London knew that Young Edward had been ceremoniously escorted from the Bishop of London's palace to lodgings in the Tower. Royal lodgings. He and Dickon shared a most splendid apartment, and a garden lay below it for their strolling and ball playing. A temporary arrangement, naturally, this Tower lodgement, to last only until His Majesty's crowning, but a most sensible one.

His Grace of Gloucester had said it well—what cheer for the Young Un and his brother at Westminster Palace these days with their lady mother, their princess sisters deserting it for the Abbey? "Taking Sanctuary" she termed it, that poor, yellow-haired Queen who so plainly had gone soft-brained with too much weeping and undue lamenting. How else explain her distraught cowering under the Abbey's protection? How else explain her openly avowed distrust for the Duke of Gloucester? For thankless she was, as well as witless, and would have naught to do with her brother-in-law despite his kindly consideration of her widowhood, his diligence in the carrying forward of plans for her son's coronation.

Not a half-bad fellow, Crook-Back, on closer acquaintance. Precisely the sort that a widowed Queen Mother and a boy king had need of in so trying an hour. Ask any man on the street, and he'd tell you the same.

The Protector. Truly, Master Pole's derisive name for Richard Plantagenet fitted him now to perfection, and one had only to look out of a window to see that the Boar's green and silver banners flew higher than any in London.

Night after night, the Council could be found in company with him, either at Baynard Castle, the House of York's family fortress on the river, or at Crosby House, his private sumptuous mansion that lay near Bishop's Gate within sound of a pleasant jangle of bells both from St. Helen's Convent of the Black Nuns and from the little Church of St. Ethelburga's.

My lords Catesby and Ratcliff and Lovel were especially favored guests. The dukes of Norfolk and Surrey and Buckingham were others who wined and dined and plotted along with a score more.

It was with the waning of May that Lord Hastings dropped away. Thomas Vaughn absented himself at the same time. Of the Stanleys, it was Sir William who appeared less frequently now.

Ecclesiastical company as well began to thin around Richard's board. The Bishop of London pleaded press of spiritual duties. John Morton of Ely sent his fine early strawberries to Richard's table, rather than his company and had taken to uneasy pacing in his garden at Holborn.

The sound of a ball striking bat was in his ears over-often.

The shouts and laughter of two blue-eyed boys playing in another garden down the Thames, below the Bridge, where the tide lapped at iron water gates and around whose high stone walls a guard of halberdiers and archers had been doubled.

May gave way to June, and June itself was a month of pageantry, of fireworks and strung-out banners, of river carnivals, of conduits running with wine, thanks to Richard's largesse, and of talk on every tongue concerning Young Edward's coronation. A month that knew a rising stir of speculation together with a bubbling foment of indignation in some quarters, lackadaisical indifference in others.

The day set for Young Edward's crowning had come and gone, with excuse upon excuse put forth from Crosby House.

Would he ever wear his golden circlet now?

But far too hot for the arguing of the question, most Londoners agreed toward the last of June when a torrid week, scorching as a blast from a forge, set in to parch them. Even the shade of its tall beech trees could not cool Master Caxton's house. On a breathless wilting night when the heat and the thump-thumping of his wooden press had driven away all hope of sleep, Peg got up from her tumbled bed, and having dressed, climbed, candle in hand, up a half flight of stairs to the Red Pale's printing loft. Anything was better than further tossing and turning. Any company preferable to her own. And she knew of a bench where she had sat more than once, having found the loft vastly diverting in the past weeks for all its head-splitting noise and its smell of printer's ink.

Master Caxton was alone, she saw, when she opened the door. With his apprentices off to bed, or more like it, bound for a tavern and a tankard of ale, he was experimenting with new leads for his press and testing their imprint on a shipment of vellum and parchment just off the wharves from Venice and Bruges.

As he worked on, bespectacled and intent, squinting in a flicker of rush light, and with no more than a nod for his midnight visitor, Peg tiptoed to her bench, and clearing it of its untidy litter, sat down. To pass the time and to forget the heat, she ruffled idly through the reams of paper stacked on the floor and now and then held a sheet up to her candle to scan the watermarks that she had learned to recognize.

A unicorn, a bull's head, a pelican, a hand-and-fleur-de-lys. And there were the letters P and Y, intricately wrought, that paid compliment to Phillip the Good of Burgundy and to Ysabelle, his wife. Patrons of letters and learning, the both of them had been.

The creamy blank sheets waiting to be fed into Master Caxton's thumping press turned Peg's thoughts toward the Christmas books whose covers she had fingered so wistfully at Ludlow Castle. Ludlow Castle. Yule-tide. The one so distant, the other so long ago. And yet neither of them out of mind for long.

What was the Princess Beth doing now, this very instant?

Was she too awake, wondering if the hot night would never drag itself to an end? Was she tossing in her bed, poisoned with her mother's suspicions and fears and wishing herself a thousand long miles, an ocean's distance from London and from Crook-Back? Or was she innocently and joyfully concerned with nothing more weighty than the planning of a new dress for her brother's oft postponed coronation? But if the day arrived at last, would she put aside her filial mourning for garments of happier hue? What color would she choose? Might her fancy light on yellow damask to match her hair? Or would she favor the azure of her eyes? Her blue, blue eyes.

Getting up from her bench, Peg wandered restlessly to a window and stared out into the muggy blackness. Faugh! Was ever so abominable a smell as the whiff of fish and tide-water rising off the sluggish river? Was ever so fetid an odor as the reek of refuse heaps and chamber-pot tossings that assaulted her nose from the narrow lanes below the casement? Given a choice, even the stench of printer's ink was far less noisome. Making a little face, Peg turned to the bench again.

Master Caxton looked up from his press. "You be sleepless, Mistress Margaret?" he inquired, unhooking his spectacles from behind his ears to breathe on them and to wipe them with a corner of the leather apron that covered his fine-tucked linen tunic. "I ben't surprised, having observed that you ate no supper. Keep on with such folly, and you'll wear yourself thin as a grass stalk! Come to think on it, I note a rumbling discontent of my own stomach. What say I rout out a servant and send round the corner to the Greyhound for a bite of sustenance? A favorite of mine, the Greyhound, as inns go. You know its oysters, its prawns? Its mustard and cress? What, never savored them? High time! And you'll join me in a sip of malmsy or sack? 'Twould do you good."

"Nay. Spare your pains, Master Caxton. A thousand thanks, but I be neither hungry nor thirsty."

Master Caxton's red-rimmed, squinting eyes probed gently. "A weight of apprehension rests upon you; be that the trouble, mistress? You have caught sight of the Boar's men who stroll past my door so oft of late? You tremble lest Richard pounce to silence your tongue from loose talk concerning Stony-Stratford?"

"I fear him day and night, Master Caxton," Peg unburdened herself. "He be a bad dream to me whether I sleep or whether my eyes be open."

"I thought it so, child. And yet where else to send you for the drawing of an easier breath? I have fretted the question more than once without finding answer. North or south, east or west, Richard could ferret you out at will. Nothing and no one would stop him now, if he so chose."

"Now? Why put it thus, Master Caxton?"

Master Caxton rubbed his spectacles to a polish and then rubbed them again and again. "You be a staunch maid," he brought out slowly, "and I must beg you to gird yourself for yet another blow. Sorry as I be to add to your dismal state, my evil tidings can wait no longer. Hear me, child. At noon this day, Richard had himself declared King. By royal proclamation he claims a fair and rightful accession to the throne, in the name of God and by consent of his Council."

"King? My uncle names himself King?"

"Small wonder that you be dazed and unbelieving, mistress. And a pity that such pure ears as yours must listen to the base presumptions that Richard flaunts. For mind you, he has smirched his own mother with the foulest of lies, swearing upon oath that his dead brother, Edward, was naught but a by-blow, born to her out of wedlock, and one whose issue thus stands barred from the throne. Further than that, without loss of an hour, he has declared Young Edward and Dickon attainted. Has ordered them moved from their state apartments. Has had them clapped into prison."

"Prison? Oh, 'tis horrible! Horrible and shameful! And what next for Young Edward and Dickon, think you, Master Caxton? Will my uncle be content to keep them in durance, or—or will he—?"

Peg's voice faltered. Her question hung in air. "Only tell me this," she stumbled on, "only tell me this, Master Caxton, what of Neddie, then, should Richard take my cousins' lives? Neddie, who be every drop as royal in blood as they?"

Master Caxton took a long time with the rehooking of his spectacles over his ears. "I would your queries were less painful, child," he admitted reluctantly. "How to answer without wounding you, when I know full well that Richard of Gloucester be a man to sweep his path clear of even the least of pebbles?"

The wooden press began to thump again.

Peg, on her bench, wished with all her heart that she knew better how to pray.

"God, keep Young Edward," was all that she could manage. "God, keep Dickon."

Then with slow tears sliding down her cheeks, she begged, "God, keep my Neddie. He be so little, God. So very little."

Chapter Eleven: A SMALL GREEN GARDEN

"Shall I be plain? I wish the bastards dead."
Richard III, Act IV, SCENE 2.

"Pies! Hot pies! Step inside. Step inside. Good pork! Good goose! And a drink of wine for the asking, masters. Red wine. White wine. Come inside. Wash the roast meat down! Cool your gullets, masters. Drink to Richard!"

Drink to Richard.

Every tavern keeper in town was shouting it from the curb by his open door. And not a pot house but swarmed with patrons raising their tankards to it and falling over themselves in a rush to swill at the Boar's trough.

Here and there, to be sure, there was a difference of opinion among such solid citizens as dyers and merchants and goldsmiths. A sword clash or two among hot-headed gentry when arguments pro or con His Grace of Gloucester grew acrimonious. Fisticuffs now and then or a street brawl when a bargeman or fishmonger or butcher took sides, calling a spade a spade. There had been a certain placard pinned up by some wag for public perusal, its verse running in this manner:

The Cat, the Rat, and Lovel the Dog,
All rule England under the Hog——

and there was little doubt as to whose names were being
played upon or what unsavory tricks their owners might be
up to. For the most part, however, Londoners were content
to shrug their shoulders. A pity, aye, that the Young Un had
lost out, but where would lie the difference a hundred years
hence—or even one? And what man, if he spoke out honestly, had a true wish to see a downy-cheeked stripling sit
the throne?

Give Crook-Back his way. Let he who could wrest a crown,
wear it, why not? 'Twould be simpler that way. Simpler and
safer, with heads being lopped the way they were these days.

Lord Rivers and Lord Grey had lost theirs at Castle Pontefract some time in June, it was known now, and Lord William Hastings had been parted from his but a short week ago.
Why? For no more than the folly of speaking out of turn
too often.

As for John Morton, Bishop of Ely, plenty of time on his
hands to ruminate belatedly upon the wisdom of keeping
one's opinions to one's self, haled off as he had been to
sternest custody.

A speedily learned lesson, these examples.

And so, on a bright brassy day early in July, while yellow-
haired Elizabeth cowered in Sanctuary, clinging to her
daughters and crying out pitifully for her sons, the Protector
had himself annointed King of England. In the splendor of
blue and cloth-of-gold doublet, his purple velvet mantle

banded and collared with miniver, his gilt spurs winking in the sunlight, he rode to the Abbey on a white prancing horse.

Outside the great carved oak doors a crowd had gathered, some among those present cheering, others silent and uncertain-eyed, a few scowling, and daring to mutter. Kneeling before the High Altar, Richard of Gloucester received the gold crown that was set upon his dark locks and stood then to take into his right hand the Orb, topped with a cross, that was held out to him by the Archbishop of Canterbury, and with his left, laid hold upon the Sceptre.

A *Te Deum* and a Mass were sung and then a feast followed in the banquet hall of Westminster Palace, a pale amber wine being passed in a jeweled loving-cup while hippocras wafers, those small spiced ceremonial cakes that were sweetened with honey from the royal hives, went the round upon a silver salver.

Richard ate and drank. My lords Catesby and Ratcliff and Lovel were in attendance on him as was Sir Henry Stafford, Duke of Buckingham, and Sir William Stanley, together with the Earls of Norfolk and Suffolk and Surrey.

Later, in his private chamber, Richard put a certain scheme before Buckingham. When he had done, a coldness lay between them. For the first time in all their mutual conniving, the Duke of Buckingham had balked. And on taking his departure from the King's apartment he was well aware that his fortunes would tumble, his head be as likely to rest upon a block as ever Lord Hastings' or any other's. 'Twas farewell, now, to further dalliance in the sun of Richard's good graces.

With his going, the King called another gentleman of the court into his chamber, Sir James Tyrrel. Here was a noble who proved of more open mind than Buckingham. For on being quizzed as to the suspected emptiness of his purse, he admitted an eager willingness to have it filled, and so was despatched upon a close-mouthed enterprise that took him to the stableyard at Crosby House. Quietly, he sought out the company of those two groomsmen whom Richard Pole had once named as John Dighton and Miles Forrest.

That same night the Duke of Buckingham rode a fast mount out of dangerous London. Casting about for some one on whom he might fawn with easier conscience than upon Richard, he turned his horse's head toward the port of Milford Haven in southern Wales.

What more likely a spot for the setting of new irons in the fire? What better chance for self-advancement than there, where a thousand other knights had already pitched their tents to wait the docking of a fateful ship from Brittany? Aboard it, so high hope and eager surmise ran, there might well be a despatch case of letters from Henry Tudor. An outline of the campaign he was rumored ready to wage.

Henry Tudor, Earl of Richmond. A man with more than one score to even. Now at last he was wearied, men said, of his over-long, stagnant dallying. With a little army of Frenchmen behind him, Frenchmen with much to gain and nothing to lose should his rising star prove no more than the bright brief flare of a rocket, he was readying himself to put fortune to the touch.

Give him arms, he was bargaining with his fellow Englishmen. Give him men. And but let them swear allegiance to the Red Rose, and Richard's downfall would be the promised coin of their repayment.

With the striking of the clock for which Sir John Manning had been listening so long, he and Master Pole were among the knights and squires who had camped on the outskirts of Milford Haven to ponder the latest news from across the sea and to argue over the Tudor's merits. Who knew him, as man to man? Not many, that was certain, with Brittany lying so far across the water.

And to back him to the hilt or not? A moot question. But what other banner to rally under now, with Young Edward's cause a lost one, Gloucester's Yorkist standard smirched with infamy?

One thing at least could be said in favor of the Tudor. Unknown quantity that he be, no man had ever named him a murderer. A murderer. Master Pole, saying the word, knew a sickness on him. Murderer. Murderer.

One hot night when he had dragged his pallet to the grass of an open meadow where a cool-sounding stream ran, he dreamt of Young Edward. Bow in hand. A quiver of arrows slung on his back. His head high. His blue eyes laughing. And Dickon beside him.

When he wakened, Master Pole lay wondering, his sorry

eyes looking out upon the summer meadow that slumbered so quietly and serenely under the white moonlight.

A day was advancing, certain as the creep of tidewater, when Richard would put Young Edward and Dickon out of his way for once and always. Who next would he set upon? And God help Mistress Margaret Plantagenet if 'twere Neddie who ran afoul of Crook-Back. Neddie, who was Mistress Margaret's very heart.

Ill-starred, hapless Mistress Margaret who, when last he had seen her, was even then a-flutter with fright. Aye, as a-flutter as Young Edward's broken-winged bird, newly caged. And yet she had known pity enough, gentleness enough, to teach the thrush to warble again, that brave and soft-mannered maid whose own glad trilling came so rarely these days and soon would be silenced for good, like as not.

When morning came, Master Pole saddled his mount and rode about the countryside seeking out the nearest friary. Having found one, he purchased a sheet of parchment for a silver piece dropped in its alms box, and then he begged use of ink and quill from a brown-hooded lay brother.

Try as he would, he could find little of cheer to write Peg. Once he had set down a brief account of himself the past months, together with a guarded hint as to what Milford Haven might hold out for the future, he would have pressed signet ring to a lump of hot wax and sealed his letter when, of a sudden, he bethought himself of something further. A sweet scent had come to his nose, and plucking a sprig of thyme from the border that rain around the friary's garden plot, he picked up his pen again. " 'Tis my hope, sweet mistress, that this bit of pungent herb will serve to carry my thoughts to you—they be manifold," he wrote. "Above all, I pray you be of good hope. An old axiom, but true, that day ever follows night."

The letter and the sprig of thyme went off to London in the pocket of a mendicant friar, its outer fold addressed to Master Caxton. It reached the city on a sweltering day in late July. Peg was in the garden when Master Caxton brought it to her. She had spent a long morning under the shade of the beech trees, a thimble on her finger and a length of Mistress Maude's snowy-bleached, sweet-smelling bed linen on her lap for a stint of hemming.

Time after time her eyes had strayed from her needle to dart one moment in search of Neddie and make quite certain that he played close to her in full sight, the next to stare beyond the garden wall and toward the river where downstream the Tower loomed.

When she had read Sir Golden Cap's letter over and over, and sniffed again and again at the little wilted sprig of thyme, she thrust them in her bodice. Overhead the parched beech trees rustled their leaves drily. Master Caxton's press thudded. Bees hummed in Mistress Maude's lavender shrubs. A faint strain of music floated from the nearby Abbey. Westminster's angelic-voiced choir boys were practicing their chorals. Listening to the high, sweet notes, with a rush of tears to her eyes, Peg seemed to hear Young Edward singing out again as he has sung so joyously, so often, in the chapel at Ludlow.

Young Edward who had been shut away in his prison chamber now for week upon week, who was denied visitors, who could neither inscribe a letter nor receive one. Master Caxton had tried and tried to send him messages of affection and cheer, and all in vain.

Poor cousin. Poor, poor uncrowned King. And poor Dickon. Poor little Duke of York.

Weighted down with pity and foreboding and listless with the heat, Peg sat under the beech trees, her sewing slipping off her lap unheeded until the Abbey bells rang out high noon, and then she stirred to send Neddie into the house to wash his face and hands and to don a clean tunic. "Remember, too, little brother, pull up your stockings and brush your hair," she admonished him. "And make my excuses at table, pray, to Mistress Maude. I ben't hungry, tell her, with the air so hot and so languid."

He ran off obediently, and in a little while Master Caxton paid a second morning visit to the garden. This time a servant followed him carrying a plate of sliced meats and bread and cheese and a foaming tankard.

"You must eat, Mistress Margaret," he urged. "You be as skinny as an eel, as sapless as a twig in winter. And drink up! What better tonic than a measure of brown ale? Be you in love; might that be your malady? 'Tis my good Maude's diagnosis, and upon my word, I think it correct. Telltale, that letter from Wales! There be a certain squire who has caught

your fancy, eh, little maid? A certain shining-locked lad?
Small wonder you moon and sigh and grow wan if naughty
Cupid has shot an arrow into your breast."

His gentle banter won a half-hearted smile and a quick
blush. And then while Peg took a bite of meat and a sip of
ale to please him, Master Caxton sat down beside her. "Will
you forgive an old man's teasing, child? 'Twas only meant
to lift your gloom in some small measure. I know full well
how trying to the spirits these days be. And a grievance to
both Mistress Maude and myself to see you so downcast, so
fearful. Not that our own reflections be less black. A most
taking way with him, your little Neddie, and the days ahead
for him a matter of gravest conjecture to us. As for Young
Edward and Dickon, have we not known them from very
cradle days? And who ever were kinder patrons to us, more
generous benefactors, than their sire, their gracious mother?"

Peg put down her plate. Her throat was dry. The meat un-
palatable.

"You see no shred of hope for them? None, Master Caxton?"

"None."

"But can no one seek audience with my uncle? Be there
no one to intercede—persuade—demand—until he listen?
And will no one rally to storm the Tower? Oh, if I were but a
man——" Peg cried it out passionately, wildly, as she had on
another day to Master Pole and Sir John Manning. "You'd
see me muster bowmen, swordsmen, see me batter gates,
scale ramparts!"

"Calm yourself, Mistress Margaret. You but lacerate yourself for naught. You but beat fists against a stone wall. Not only one, but a very sheaf of petitions have already been scorned by Gloucester. And whenever did the Tower give way to assault? Would it now, then? I think not, child. And painful as it be, the cold truth stares us in the face. Their prison chamber holds your cousins fast. In the Tower they be, and in the Tower they'll die. 'Tis writ for anyone to see. Writ large. Writ clear."

The parched leaves rustled overhead. The bees hummed in their honied shrubs. The choir boys sang louder from the Abbey stalls, a good dinner having been downed in the refectory. Young Edward's thrush, perched in the wicker cage that was hung on the ivied garden wall, trilled rapturously, his sweet notes soaring with theirs, up and up and up.

The two on the bench had fallen into a sorry musing silence but all at once Master Caxton jumped up, clapping hand to forehead, his eyes snapping behind their spectacles. "I have it!" he exclaimed, clutching hold of Peg's arm. "I have it, child! Those chorals wafting from yonder, and your thrush warbling, have struck me all of a heap. Both shall serve a purpose, a mighty purpose!"

He had pulled Peg to her feet now. "You hear the choir? Then mind you, there be nary a church in London but boasts the like, be it small or large, for the chanting of its offices, its matins, its vespers. Nary a one, I say, and not excepting St. Peter's ad Vinicula that stands upon the Tower Green. The Tower Green, child!"

Master Caxton shook Peg as though she slept, heavily.
"Wake up! Wake up! Where be your wits? Where be your
grasp of this chance held out? Though I myself be a dummy
not to have latched to it earlier—and pray Heaven, pray God
in His goodness, 'tis not too late even now."

"Too late? But for what, Master Caxton?"

"Come. Wake up, did you hear me? And have done with
gaping at me. Your wits, I say, child, your wits! Gather them
swiftly. Be you with me? Then hark close, and speak your
mind freely as to whether or not my words carry a feasible
ring. What say you to a priest seen sauntering through the
Tower Wards, shortly after evensong, let us say, and in company with two youths, hooded and cassocked and carrying
each of them a psalter, as befits choir boys? Would they be
halted, think you at the Tower gates, or more likely be
granted egress at will?"

"Egress? A holy priest? Two cassocked youths?" Peg repeated it bewilderedly, and then a great wave of understanding broke over her. "Master Caxton! Oh, good, kind Master
Caxton! Clever Master Caxton! A most splendid plan. Never
did I dream the like. But the risk? The awful danger? You'd
dare so brave a try?"

"Why not? And no need to speak of valiance, Mistress
Margaret. Rather, credit me with but a decent gratitude
for past favors—a deep affection, a heartfelt pity. But now
to ways and means. Before all else I shall have need of a
trusted helpmate. But not you, little maid. Nay, I'll not listen
to you. 'Twould be sheerest folly to embroil you. So save

your breath, for I be adamant. Let me but ponder a moment."

Master Caxton's peering near-sighted eyes went reflectively to the wicker cage that hung on the garden wall. "Methinks I have it. The very thing! Tell me, Mistress, what of that ancient toothless beldame who accompanied you from Ludlow Castle? Be she loyal to Young Edward in your judgement?"

"Beyond all doubt, Master Caxton. For though she be crusty and rough tongued, she has served the Royal Household for year upon year, putting hand to broom and mop in the nursery when first the Princess Beth was born."

"And would welcome a chance to lend aid toward Young Edward's freeing, you think?"

"I be certain of it. Certain."

"Excellent. None could suit my purpose better. Her name —Susan Dow? She must be fetched from the palace at once. As to what shall follow, I can give you but the briefest notion. My plans will burgeon fully only when I see the lay of the land, you understand. But for a beginning, you must know that the Tower, so called, is in itself a veritable lair of Towers. There be twelve in all. That particular one in which your cousins be now secured, receives its name of Garden House from a green plot, high-walled, that lies behind its portcullis. And though I have no certain knowledge, what more reasonable to suppose that there be a tree or two shading it? Trees under whose branches a pair of youthful prisoners might stroll of a summer evening perchance, were they granted leave to stretch limb before bedtime set in upon them. Trees from whose boughs a length of tossed rope might conceivably dangle. But more of that anon, child. More anon——"

Master Caxton broke off to glance at the sky. The brassy glare that had blistered London for days was gone. There was a sullen leaden look to it now. The air was heavy and oppressive and without faintest stir. The beech leaves hung motionless, stilled the past few minutes, and with their rustle gone from them.

"A thunderstorm brewing, from the look of it," he announced with satisfaction. "And all the better for my scheming should it break. Let rain pelt the Tower with the coming on of evening, and nary a guard but will scurry to barrack room and sentry box. Fewer curious eyes, less sharp ones, will be turned upon a wet bedraggled priest and his young choristers hurrying out the gate toward home and dry garb and a hot supper."

"You mean to venture to the Tower this very day, Master Caxton?"

"This very hour even. You think there be so much as a sole precious moment to lose? Not a one. The sand in your cousin's hourglass runs out all too quickly. I be off at once to the Abbey to borrow vestments. Little difficulty to the transaction, I fancy—the choirmaster be an old acquaintance of mine. I've struck off chant and anthem for him more than a few times on my press. For your part, mistress, take wing swiftly. Fly in search of my wife. Relate to her all that we have touched upon and say I bid her send for Susan Dow without delay. And see to it that the woman be cloaked and ready to set out with me immediately upon my return."

Master Caxton took hurried departure from his garden, leaving Peg with half a hundred questions on her lips, her heart beating fast, her gray eyes shining with quick-springing hope.

Crook-Back bested at long last. His perfidy, his baseness an open book. London willing now to read, and to draw sword against him. Young Edward truly King. Oh, a thousand, thousand times better late than never, his triumphant donning of a crown! Thank you, dear Lord in Heaven! Thank you! For what else, the portent of Young Edward's golden circlet than a blessed ring of safety cast round Neddie?

The leaden sky, darker now, lowered ominously as Peg raced to the house to seek Mistress Maude. Beading of perspiration was on her upper lip as she ran, her linen shift clung moist against her body, her russet curls matted damply on her forehead. The heat. The breathless heat. Like a pall, it lay over all London.

At the stables of Crosby House, Master Caxton's talk of a storm was being echoed by two other men who found high satisfaction in the promise of a wet dark night.

John Dighton and Miles Forrest, having scraped manure from their boots and put on clean livery, sallied forth to the riverside tavern where Sir James Tyrrel had taken pleasant abode. Sir James Tyrrel, that nobleman so recently penniless, so newly rich.

While he waited their arrival and dallied with a supper of

partridge pie and a bottle of finest ruby-red Gascoigny wine, Sir James was fingering an iron key and a scrap of paper on which a password had been scribbled. My lord Robert Brakenbury, High Constable of the Tower of London, had been commanded to slip both of them into Sir James' hand.

Chapter Twelve: MIDNIGHT

"The tyrannous and bloody deed is done—"
Richard III, Act IV, SCENE 3.

The London drought was over. About five o'clock in the afternoon the rain began to fall in big slow lukewarm drops. Susan Dow felt the first splatter of them as she shuffled through the Outer Ward of the Tower and took the cobbled walk that led to Young Edward's and Dickon's prison.

The gray sullen river and a wharf, its steps slimy with moss and set with iron mooring rings, lay on her right. A high blank stone wall reared on her left.

"Hold, beldame!"

The sharp command rang out just before she reached the iron-toothed portcullis that barred entrance to the Inner Ward and to the Garden Tower.

"Hold, I say!" A scarlet-hosed blue-doubleted yeoman, lounging outside his sentry box, had sprung to the alert. "Hold, in the name of the King!"

With a startled jump and an outraged screech, Susan Dow came to an abrupt halt, the tickle of a halberd point against her cloaked ribs.

"I heard you, Master Warder. I heard you. No need to shout. No need to scare a body out of his wits. I ben't deaf. Nay, nor a pig to be stuck! Look to that steel of yours and oblige me by stepping back a bit, will you, Lobster Legs?"

"Lobster Legs, eh? Then it's Mother Drip Nose to you, my friend. But speak out, and in a hurry. What be your business in the Royal Ward?"

"The handing over of Master Chirp here to Young Edward, granted your kind leave." Susan Dow held up the wicker cage she was carrying. "Have a gander if you will. 'Tis a broken-winged thrush that His Highness once picked off the moor at Ludlow. Took a fancy to it, he did, and made a pet of it."

"And how come you by it, old crone?"

"Easy enough to answer. Ben't I in service at the palace? And haven't I fetched and carried for His Highness since the day he first suckled? Who more likely then to bring his little twittering birdie to him, knowing he be shut behind bars, poor sweet lamb, and in so dire a need of cheering?"

"But who passed you through the Outer Bailey, tell me that, will you? Who gave you permit beyond the Middle Tower?"

"A warder not half so handsome as you, pretty boy, but one with a heart in his breast all the same. 'Trot along, grandam,' was what he said when I told him where I was bound, 'and good luck to you at the Garden Tower. Young Edward and his brother can do with a bit o' brightness, it strikes me—cruel it was, locking them up in a prison chamber.' Those be his very words, Lobster Legs. His very words."

"And he spoke for others beside himself, come to think on it."

The halberd point was drawn back an almost imperceptible sixteenth of an inch from Susan Dow's ribs and she let out her breath in audible relief. Then because the raindrops had begun to pelt a little harder, she pulled her cloak around her and made a great to-do of attempting to cover the wicker cage as well.

"By St. Anne, how it pours! Did ever see the like? You'll do me a favor, Lobster Legs, and carry his thrush to Young Edward before its feathers be wet down? And no further dawdling, I pray you, or I'll catch my death standing here. Kerchoo! Kerchoo! You hear that? Have you no pity for a poor old woman kept out in such weather? Come now, say you'll take the birdie to Young Edward, there's a good lad. Did ever a kind deed go amiss? And don't forget, handsome be as handsome does, so soften up, Lobster Legs, soften up! Why not, for where lies the smallest harm in His Majesty having Master Chirp for company, that's what I'd like to know?"

The rain had become a torrent while Susan Dow wheedled and sneezed and snuffled. Thunder rumbled over the river. A jagged streak of lightning cut the sky. As it flashed, a clock struck somewhere inside the Garden Tower.

Susan Dow squeezed a little stream of water from her cloak hem. "You'll see? I be dripping, pretty boy. And look at my birdie, will you? Fair drowned! And all of it fault of yours that we stand here with buckets emptying upon our noggins. Aye, your blame alone that Master Chirp and I be shivering and drenched."

"Your whining and sniveling grow tedious, Mother Drip Nose. What concern of mine if your bird gets a bath? But give it me, give it me, if so doing will rid me of you both."

The yeoman plucked the cage from Susan Dow. "You heard the clock, did you? It be the supper hour. And if I see to it that Young Edward has his thrush served up with his mug and trencher, will you take yourself off?"

"Quicker than quick, I promise you. And my thanks, thrice over." Susan Dow fumbled under her cloak and pulled out a small, muslin sack. "One more favor from you, Lobster Legs—millet seed for Master Chirp. And will you bid Young Edward look to the filling of his birdie's water cup? 'Tis as dry as cuttlebone, having sloshed empty as I journeyed from Westminster. You'll surely put His Highness in mind of it? You'll not let it slip your memory? You'll make it clear to him that his thrush be woefully parched and like as not more dead than alive for want of a drink?"

"Ha! Parched, is he now, your Master Chirp? Methought him drowning but a moment past. Make up your mind, Gammer Hoddy-Doddy! Make up your mind."

A few minutes later when Susan Dow, cackling slyly to herself, her black eyes agleam with satisfaction, had gone her way through the pelting wind-driven rain, a jailer was climbing the steep stairs that wound to the Upper Chamber of the Garden Tower.

Unlocking an iron-banded oak door, he entered and set down a tray and a bird cage on a trestle table.

"Your supper, young masters," he announced. "What's more a songster for you. Sent up it were by order of the Yeoman of the Portcullis. Here be seed for it in this sack. And mind you give it a drink, first thing, I was to tell you."

Having lifted the lid from a platter that gave off the steam of hot meat, he took his departure.

Young Edward, standing by a narrow slit in the stone wall and gazing moodily into the small green court below, had paid little or no attention to him, but Dickon, playing on the floor with a battalion of painted lead soldiers, scrambled to his feet and filled with eager curiosity, ran to the table.

"What did the fellow mean, brother? A songster? For us? From whence did it come, think you? Who could have sent it? But look! Look! I do believe—yes! Come see for yourself! 'Tis your very own thrush from Ludlow."

Young Edward whirled from the window. "Mine?" For a moment he could only stare incredulously, and then he ran to the table as eagerly as Dickon and hurried to unlatch the cage door.

At his coaxing chirrup, the thrush hopped out, dragging its broken wing in the old familiar manner, and perched upon Young Edward's outstretched hand as comfortably and as much at home as though it were tilting on a hedge twig.

Preening its feathers, cocking a bright eye, it began to trill.

"You remember me, do you, little caroler, even though so long a while has passed since last we met? Nor have I forgotten you. But how did you find me? Who fetched you here?"

As he asked his questions, Young Edward stroked the thrush and held it close against his shabby velvet tunic. "I would that you had tongue for speech as well as song," he half whispered. "Yes, my small and faithful friend, for there be more queries than one that I have longing to put."

"And if your bird could speak, brother, would he tell us when we may leave this dreary place, think you?" Dickon's eyes were wistful as the thrush flooded the grim bare room with a song that was like the pouring out of so much sweet pure water. "Could he tell us why we have had to stay on and on so very long a while, disliking this Tower chamber as we do?"

"And you think we have need of a bird to answer such questions?"

Young Edward's head went into the air with a toss that he managed to make both haughty and superior. "What a baby you be, Dickon! Will you never get it clear that we lodge here only until the waiting for my coronation comes to an end?"

"Ye—s. But a most irksome lingering, no matter what its reason. It wearies me, brother. I want to go home. I detest these walls. Why do they close round us so harsh and so gray? Why be we shut in so alone? Why does no one come to see us? And why the bolt upon our door? Why its key?"

"Did ever see door without one? And have I not explained time and time again our lack of visitors? 'Tis natural enough, their absence. Take for example the question of our Uncle Richard. How expect to see him, occupied as he be from morn till night with the shaping of arrangements for my crowning? And as for our lady mother, must I dwell again upon the piteous grief that warps her days?"

"But where be Beth? Where be Cecily?"

"Where else but at the palace, and as caught up in grief as our mother, foolish Dickon. And is it the hundredth or the thousandth time that I have told you 'tis ever the way of women to keep to themselves aloof and apart when they weep?"

"But, what of our other uncle? What of Lord Rivers? Where be he?"

Young Edward hesitated. "That, I know not for certain," he admitted slowly. "Let us say he has gone to Ludlow."

"And be Cousin Margaret and Neddie with him, think you?"

"There be little reason to doubt it."

"And Master Pole, where be he?"

"At Ludlow, too, with Sir John Manning, why not, as I have told you and told you and told you?"

"But—but I do not understand. If all of them be so far away, brother, who then sent you your thrush?"

"How say, with his coming as much a riddle to me as to you? But here he be, and so why bother our heads with questions? Rather, let us pull up to the table before our meat grows cold. I've no palate for a congealed and lardlike supper, have you?"

Young Edward shut the thrush in its cage, and he and Dickon sat down and filled their pewter trenchers with food from the tray.

There were slices of beef, floating in gravy, a loaf of bread, a wedge of yellow cheese, a plum tart, a beeker of wine and one of water.

As they lifted their mugs, Young Edward suddenly and remorsefully bethought him of the jailer's admonition to give his bird a drink. Jumping up, he opened the cage door and pulled out its little water cup. Holding it under the lip of the beeker, he was about to pour, when his blue eyes widened, startled and unbelieving.

The water cup, though indeed as dry as cuttlebone, was not empty. A tiny pellet of rolled-up paper had been stuck to the bottom of it with a drop of wax. Snatching at it, smoothing out its creases, Young Edward read its single line.

"In the garden, this day, at vespers."

There was no signature, but below the lettering in one corner, a tiny red shield had been sketched and a small flower, yellow-centered with the raying petals of a daisy.

A daisy? Nay! A Marguerite. His Cousin Peg's namesake flower, no less. And what else, that little shield, but Master Caxton's very own Red Pale? Or was he but guessing? Clutching at a straw? Hoping with all his longing heart?

YOUNG EDWARD READ ITS SINGLE LINE.

No. No. It had to be. It had to be. Succor was here at last!

Dizzy with joy, beside himself with wild excitement, Young Edward wanted to laugh out loud, gladly, triumphantly, as he had not laughed for months. He wanted to hug Dickon. He wanted to wrestle with him. To roll on the floor. To shout gleefully and triumphantly. To cry out his tidings so that all of London might hear. All of England. All of the Kingdom that was to be his again.

But nay. Time now for a hold on himself. Time now for steadiness and for calm and careful reasoning, planning.

He grasped Dickon's arm. "Listen well, little brother. A thing has come to pass that will make you glad—glad! And we shall be leaving this ugly lonesome chamber sooner than I had thought. But not a question from you at the moment. Not a one!"

While Dickon stared, his round eyes bewildered, a mouthful of hot plum tart silencing him more effectually than any command, Young Edward turned again to the arrow-slit.

Every inch of the muddy, rain-deluged garden that lay below was known to him. He and Dickon had sought it out day after day, all summer long, grateful for a chance to stretch their legs, grateful for a breath of air that was fresher far, despite the stifling heat, than that of their musty-smelling damp-walled prison.

Even on the hottest days, the garden had been shaded at its far end by the overhanging leafy branch of a giant wytch elm that was rooted just outside the wall.

A stout branch—Young Edward eyed it consideringly, his heart lurching and pounding with ever-growing hope. A branch that arched some twenty feet above the garden's greensward. Yes, a good twenty feet. But with the aid of a tossed rope, a cleated or knotted rope, could two strong agile boys not swing themselves up onto it? And once straddling it, hidden in deep foliage, could they not manage to clamber down, from limb to limb, and land safely upon the other side of the wall? That beckoning tantalizing other side, facing upon the open Tower Yard where lay a chance, at very least, for freedom?

They could. They could, he and Dickon, with all the ease in the world.

And that was what Master Caxton and Peg meant them to do. That was what the symbol of the Red Pale and the symbol of the Marguerite were trying to say. Somehow, someway, they had hit upon a plan, those two. A very marvel of a plan. He knew it. He knew it. No slightest doubt shadowed his grasp of it.

Once again, Young Edward longed to shout out loud, longed to throw his arms around Dickon in a jubilant hug. It was cold, sober reality that checked him abruptly.

Oh, heartless Heaven, cruel Heaven, to have loosed a flood upon this of all days!

How, with the afternoon so wet, gain permission from their jailer for a stroll in the garden? Would he not scoff, and declare them daft, should they plead for an airing before night closed in?

Worse, would suspicion not stir in his breast at the proposal of an outing in the pouring rain? And what then, if the wall were all at once set round with sentries? Might not Master Caxton himself be snared, if indeed he waited there now, secret and hidden beyond the elm's thick trunk?

And yet nothing for it but to seize upon this glorious chance. How hesitate, with the day almost done, with twilight at hand, with the vesper hour waiting only to be rung?

A mutter of thunder, a blinding flash of lightning made Young Edward flinch from the arrow-slit, but despite it, he turned to Dickon, his decision made.

"Cloak yourself, and at once, my brother. Have done with supper! Put spoon and knife aside. The tart can wait. I be in favor of a run in the garden. 'Tis all too close inside here, and sticky as treacle. You see how my tunic clings? Methinks a cooling-off and breath of air will let us sleep the better when we later seek our beds. What say? You be for it?"

"A hundredfold and over!"

Dickon's face lighted. Shoving back from the table, he ran to a wooden chest that stood against the wall and dragged out a brown velvet cape that was edged round with softest martin fur and a matching cap, rakish with a pheasant quill thrust aslant its brim, rich with the glitter of its Duke of York's gold rose.

Young Edward threw his own cloak around him and donned a cap from which three white plumes drooped. Imperiously then, he pounded on the iron-banded oak door.

When at last he made himself heard above the rumble of

thunder that was growing louder with every peal, and when the door had been unlocked, he faced the jailer with his head high, his bearing princely.

"We be bound for a stroll in the garden," he announced. "You will see to the unbarring of the lower story at once. And be quick about it, good keeper, if you please. 'Twill be dark should we delay our airing much longer."

He spoke as cooly and as matter-of-factly as though a perfect summer evening lay waiting his royal enjoyment, filled expressly by his order with the soft rustle of leaves and the fresh smell of grass and of the open air.

Goggling at him, the jailer pushed an ear forward, more than a little uncertain as to his hearing. "What say, young sir, what say? A turn in the garden? Be you jesting with me? Hark to the thunder! And as for the rain, another cloud-burst and the Tower itself will float away. Even now the whole of the Yard be awash, and the grass plot below naught but a mud puddle, a duck pond."

"And if such the case, all the more sport in store for us," Dickon broke in delightedly. "We shall play at being drakes, my brother and I. We shall splash and paddle like veritable water fowl! Watch me, Master Keeper. 'Twill be something in this manner, our progress——"

Laughing, his eyes merry, Dickon squatted down, turning out his feet as though they were flat and webbed, and waddled comically back and forth across the Upper Chamber's threshold.

"Would you spoil his fun, fellow? Why not heed him?

Why not grant him access to the garden?" Young Edward's voice was urgent now, and pleading rather than arrogant. "I beg it of you. Be there other amusement offered by the Tower to wile away the hours for one so few in years? Nay, none. And the very toys he plays with are broken for the most part after all these weary months. And what matter, a drop or two of rain upon our heads? Do we stand in danger of melting, think you?"

"Have it your way, young sir. Do as you please, for all of me. Splash your fill! But 'twill be your rheum, and none of mine, when you come dripping back, sneezing and hawking and calling out for a rub of goose grease on your wheezy windpipes."

With a shrug then, the jailer led a way down the winding stone stair and turning left at the bottom, halted at a grilled iron door that was sunk in the wall of a narrow passageway. Rattling his keys, he unlocked it and flung it open. "Mind you, be you drakes or not, I shall wait you here in no more than minutes. Let vespers strike, and in you come, on the run. Enough is enough, and a little goes a long way, as you'll find out when you begin to shiver in soggy boots and soaked mantles."

Before the grilled door swung shut, and while the jailer's grumbled warning was still upon his lips, another clap of thunder reverberated directly over the Garden Tower. It was twice as loud and ominous as any that had echoed before.

The gray sky was suddenly illuminated with a livid flare. A zigzag of lightning had cut across it, bright as fire. Its sizzling blast struck the giant wytch elm. The high overhanging branch split away from its trunk, seared and jagged. A mightier crash followed. The whole of the tree toppled and with its twisted writhing boughs down went a rubble of bricks from the top of the garden wall.

Of the three who stood by the grilled door, Young Edward was the first to speak.

"Come," he commanded Dickon from the depths of a numbing and bitter despair. "Come. Back to our chamber. Master Keeper spoke the truth—an unpropitious evening for a stroll. Not one that I would have chosen."

Without another word, he began to climb the stone stairs.

The Upper Chamber lay in gloomy darkness now, with a lash of rain against its thick walls and with the arrow-slit no more than a frame for shadows.

Leaning against the deep-set embrasure, Young Edward took up his moody staring, his eyes on nothing.

The jailer, lighting a candle in a pewter stick, picked up the supper tray and closed the door behind him.

The key turned in the lock. The bolt shot into its socket. And with the sound of footsteps dying away, the vesper bells began to ring.

Dong! Dong!

Ding-dong! Ding-dong!

Little Dickon pulled off his cap and tossed it in a corner, and let his cape fall to the floor. "Was it fair, brother, your giving up our game?" he questioned aggrievedly. "Not to my mind! And why so sudden a change of heart? Why so swift a loss of zest for our playing of drakes? Was it the crackle and crash that frightened you? For shame, such cowardice! Was I afraid? Nay. And yet I be not near so old as you."

"True—but braver by far, methinks." Young Edward turned from the window. "I little knew a clap of thunder, a flash of lightning could so undo me. But 'tis over now, and done with." He threw off his cloak, and the cap with the three white plumes joined Dickon's in a careless heap. "I be sorry truly to have spoilt your paddling. What of a game of soldiers to take its place? Would it please you if I helped you set out your tents, helped you range pikemen and archers in battle order?"

The two of them sprawled on the stone floor manoeuvering an army of battered lead knights and henchmen until Dickon began to yawn and yawn and yawn.

Wishing pleasant dreams to the thrush, already asleep in its cage, its head tucked under a wing, he undressed, pulled on a white linen nightshift and knelt by a canopied bed to say his prayers. When he had come to the end of them, he climbed under the covers.

"Would you be provoked with me, brother, if I asked but one small question?" he wanted to know, his eyes bright with curiosity. " 'Tis concerning the bit of paper that was sealed in your bird's water cup. Was there not writing upon it of sorts?"

"Yes. Writing that carried greetings to us from kind Master Caxton of the Red Pale and from our Cousin Peg, who, I take it has found lodging there for the nonce. Greetings, mind you, that promised we shall see them soon." Young Edward's voice was quiet and steady as he answered Dickon.

"But was it a secret, brother, their message? Was it to be a surprise? Is that why you confide it to me only now, so tardily?"

"True, 'twas a secret, Dickon."

"And when we be together with them, will they have news for us of our lady mother? Will we see her, as well, think you? And Beth and Cecily and our Cousin Neddie and all the others of our family? I long to, exceedingly much, brother."

"And so you shall—but all in good time, and off to sleep with you, at the moment."

Young Edward, in turn, undressed and donned night clothes. He said his prayers. He blew out the candle.

Lying in bed with Dickon curled close, he found himself putting question after question to the darkness that closed them in. What might the morrow bring? Another chance to leave their prison? Would Master Caxton make a second try to free them? Could he? But how, how?

And what was the true meaning, the inner core of Master Caxton's and Peg's daring message? What was its portent? Was danger pressing so hard now, peril so close, that none but the most flimsy of schemes, the most rash of ventures could have held hope of saving Dickon and himself?

Saving them? Saving them from what? From what and from whom?

"Be you asleep, brother?" The small curled hump lying

next to Young Edward stirred under its quilt. "Will the wind have done with its howling presently, think you?" Dickon was asking in an uneasy whisper. "Will the thunder cease? The rain give up its drumming? I trust so—'tis difficult getting off to slumber with so loud a din in my ears. And perchance I be as great a coward as you after all, for I find I have little fancy for the lightning that flashes so burning bright through our window. Will you not tell me a story to pass the night? Do, brother. Do, please."

"A story? And what tale shall it be?"

"The chronicle of how you chanced upon your thrush lying all frozen and broken-winged upon the moor at Ludlow and of how it found its song once more—'tis a favorite of mine, that."

"As well I know. And if you close your eyes, you shall have it again."

Young Edward put an arm around Dickon, and Dickon's yellow locks fell with his against their pillow. "Once upon a time, not so long ago," Young Edward began, "when white new snow heaped the land, and when the season of Yule was drawing nigh, a certain Prince might have been seen striding across a moor that lay in the shadow of a strong and beautiful castle. A castle where a King and Queen and their happy children lived——"

The story wound to its close. Long after Dickon's soft even breathing told that he was asleep, Young Edward lay awake, pondering once more upon the morrow.

The morrow. Surely, surely it would dawn in brightness?

The storm would be spent? And the floating doubts, the horrid black mistrust that tormented him would have subsided,
just as the muddy water would have drained away from the
green garden outside? To doubt it would to be lost in a very
swamp of terror. Naught but a figment of the night were the
foolish qualms that beset him now. Nothing more. Nothing
more.

And yet, those warnings of his Cousin Peg—what of them?
And what of a pair of eyes, seen for himself to be those of
a toad's? Lest the dreadful fear that clutched him prove his
master, Young Edward made himself remember that he was
King.

King of England, with a golden crown awaiting him in
the Abbey. An orb. A sceptre. A throne. No one could deny
them to him. No one could strip them from him. No one
would dare. No one at all. Not even—not even. . . .

He had fallen asleep with Dickon locked fast in his arms,
when with the coming of midnight, the bells of St. Peter's
ad Vinicula rang out from the Tower Green.

Dong! Dong!

Ding, dong!

The thunder had ceased. The rain had abated; the wind
calmed. All the Garden Tower lay in silence.

Then slowly an oiled bolt was drawn from its socket. A
key was cautiously turned in a lock. Noiselessly, the door to
the Upper Chamber swung open.

Two cloaked and hooded figures with the smell of a stable
about them slipped into the room. Halting for a moment,

they peered quickly through the darkness. One stiffled a curse when he knocked against the trestle table, then they stole toward the canopied bed.

A thick smothering quilt was pulled high. A suffocating pillow was pressed down, down.

When the bells of St. Peter's ad Vinicula rang again, this time for matins, Young Edward's thrush woke in its wicker cage and, glad of the shaft of sunlight that struck through the arrow-slit, swelled its white throat and began to sing.

There was no one to hear its morning choral.

The Upper Chamber was empty.

But at the foot of the steep winding stair, close to the wall, there was a drip of candle wax. A stone panel bore a chisel mark. And a trace of loose mortar and fresh earth showed where a grave had been hastily dug and as hastily closed.

Chapter Thirteen: A STROLL ALONG
THE RIVER

"The chaplain of the Tower has buried them;
But how, or in what place I do not know."
Richard III, Act IV, SCENE 3.

September.

Purple asters starred the roadside ditches. Blue borage veined the meadows. White campion foamed under the feet of wayfarers. And on a day that hinted of coming frost and of yellowing, falling leaves, Richard Pole rode into London from Milford Haven bent upon the carrying of letters and word-of-mouth news to a little knot of Lancastrians with whom Sir John Manning was in correspondence.

He had gone about his business quietly and discreetly, and his mission was completed. Now there was the shank of the afternoon left him for a call upon Master Caxton and Mistress Maude. And time, it proved agreeably, for a little stroll with Peg.

Taking a turfy green path to the river, they sat down on the bank to watch the white swans that floated by and the flight of duck and crane and goose against the blue of the cold clear sky.

Peg had picked a nosegay of late hedgerow flowers as they strolled, and now, twisting a Michaelmas daisy between her fingers, her glance turned away from Sir Golden Cap, she asked with a wistfulness that could not be disguised, "You must take your departure on the morrow, you say, Master Pole? There be no chance of a longer stay in London?"

"None, Mistress Margaret." Sir Golden Cap picked up a pebble and tossed it into the water. "Sir John waits my immediate return. I hope, however, to dally more leisurely on some future day if all goes well."

"Your absence will be a lengthy one?"

" 'Tis difficult to say at the moment and depends largely upon this and that and the other thing, mistress, with the fortunes of war, the hazards of the field to be considered."

"The Tudor strikes a blow soon, did I hear you confide to Master Caxton?"

"He'll strike, right enough, aye, but as to when, that be a different story altogether. Troops and arms and mounts be not so easily come by, you understand. A cautious man, the Tudor, if ever were. Wary and cool and forward-looking. You think he'd risk his skin without full complement of bowmen and pikemen and swordsmen assured him? Not he! A very fox for shrewdness and bargaining."

" 'Twill be months, then, you think, before he lands and marches?"

"A year, rather. Two, should ill winds blow his plans awry as they've done before, worse luck."

"Two years?" Peg echoed it, dismayed. "And you'll wait

him all that while in Milford Haven? A long long time indeed."

"True. There be no gainsaying it, Mistress Margaret."

Wordless and meditative, they watched the river and the white swans, and then Sir Golden Cap, chewing on a grass stalk, observed reflectively, "Let two years pass before I return, and I shall have gained knighthood, it occurs to me. And with squireship fully served and put behind me, I shall be my own master."

"So?" Peg pulled at her daisy. "As for me, Master Pole, I shall have gone forward, too, and be well into my fifteenth year."

Again there was a meditative silence. Peg plucked at her daisy petals. Master Pole tossed another pebble. After that, looking up at the sun, he declared it time to turn back to the sign of the Red Pale. He helped Peg to her feet, she brushed a lady bird and a twig from her gray skirt, and then as they walked along, he asked her about her plans for the coming winter.

"You will stay on at Master Caxton's dwelling, you and Neddie?"

"Where else to go, Master Pole? Where else to turn?"

"But surely you be happy, you be content with Master Caxton and Mistress Maude?"

"Happy? Content? Alas, the words hold little meaning for me, though I beg you not to find me ungrateful, Master Pole. Never has such kindness been showered upon me since I lost my mother and sire, I swear. And my own fault alone that the days here hold so little cheer."

"It be your old fear of Crook-Back that darkens them, that pricks you sharp as ever, Mistress Margaret?"

" 'Tis no prick, Master Pole. A stab, rather. And call me coward if you will for cringing under it, call me lily-livered, call me a fool; I cannot help myself. The most dire imaginings cloud round me. They flock like dismal ravens, cawing and cawing, and blackening every moment."

"A pity, mistress. I be sorry for you. And yet to my mind you torment yourself unduly. As I look upon it, there be a brighter tinge to your immediate prospects than for some while past. If Gloucester meant harm to you or Neddie, would he not have swooped by now? What to stay him? What to hold him off? Naught, so far as I can see."

"So Master Caxton argues, even though he himself was as apprehensive as I not long ago. But now he declares it clear as day that our uncle has brushed us from mind as not worth second thought. Easy enough for him to forget us, Master Caxton avers, with his crown firm, as he fancies, and with all of London held in the palm of his hand. What's more, all of England, so he boasts. Was ever such vainglory, such conceit? Puffed with pride as an adder, he be. Have you heard how he scoffs, how his lips twist in that thin sneering smile of his when the Tudor's name be spoke?"

"Aye. He rides a high horse, Crook-Back. And a fond

hope among us at Milford Haven that he'll take a fall one fine day. But tell me more of Master Caxton's views, mistress. It be his firm belief that Gloucester has chosen to ignore you for the nonce?"

"So he vows most solemnly. But be it only to cheer me, think you, Master Pole? Or might it be true? Oh, to have it so! Neddie and I awakening, then, each morning and knowing that we be safe. Closing our eyes at nightfall and savoring security even in the dark. Believe me, Master Pole, 'tis my every longing, my every prayer."

"And shall be mine from henceforth, Mistress Margaret."

Sir Golden Cap said it simply and warmly, looking down at Peg out of steady hazel eyes.

They had reached Master Caxton's doorway; he bade her good day with a reminder that he would be back to speak his final farewell early the next morning and with a regret that he could not linger for the refreshment of cake and fruit and mead that she offered.

"But the repast will be set out waiting, Master Pole. Mistress Maude and Master Caxton commanded me to bring you in without fail. A disappointment to Neddie, also, unless you stay. And—and one to me."

"You think I refuse your hospitality willingly, Mistress Margaret? Nay, far from it. But I shall be late in arrival at the Abbey if I stay to break bread, and as the hour for my visit was set by Her Majesty's Lady-in-Waiting, I must keep it promptly. I go to offer homage to the Queen and Prin-

cess Beth and to carry them my compassion. Unfortunate
sorrowing ladies, they have indeed been hounded with grief
and mischance since last I saw them."

"But you run no risk, seeking out the Queen so openly, so
boldly? You have no fear of Richard's henchmen laying
hands upon you?"

"None. Why should I? Who knows me from a hundred
other squires riding the streets at will, going hither and
thither as they choose? And who pray would trouble to halt
me? Who would trouble to inquire my business, question
my loyalties? Not the King himself, I'll warrant, even
though we rode head on to one another at the palace's very
gate—though I own to no inordinate wish to put it to test,
you understand, Mistress Margaret! But jesting aside, I be
like you and Neddie these days, methinks, with the three of
us less in importance than a gnat sting to Crook-Back. Neddie's rights of inheritance are flouted as beneath notice. Your
implication and mine in the affair at the Lamp and Wick,
and my allegiance to Sir John of lighter weight than a
feather to him. And there's yet another explanation for what
you mistakenly term my boldness in riding the streets—ben't
Gloucester absent from town? I have heard it so."

"There be no telling, Master Pole. His banner flies from
the palace whether he stays or goes, and he has taken to
shuttling back and forth out of London with greatest fre-
quency these days."

"He rides to the north, does he, bent on the drumming-up of fealty in a shire or two that lack affection for him? And tosses bones, I take it, where'er they'll be gnawed with proper slavering, proper gratitude?"

" 'Tis the current talk, true enough, Master Pole. Though whether he gains a further following or not no one knows beyond a guess. Opinion on the subject shifts. One day, Master Caxton and his friends shudder to hear that he grows in favor mightily, thanks to those tossed bones you speak of, and then upon the very next, they rejoice mightily over rumors that speak of a marked and growing repugnance toward him. But where the truth lies—has any man the answer?" Peg glanced toward the river as she spoke, and along its bank as though she could see the Tower. "The answer to anything, Master Pole? And how many many questions there be! But my apologies to you. I delay you over long. You must take your leave."

When Master Pole had ridden away, Peg crossed the hall and began to climb the stairs to her bedchamber.

Once more, she knew that curious swelling, nay, that nigh to bursting, 'twould seem, of her heart. That pain beneath her bodice that had become a frequent visitor of late.

Princess Beth—so good, so fair, so piteous, and so deserving of—of—of everything worth having in all the world.

She had reached the first landing when Master Caxton and Mistress Maude caught the flick of her skirt and called to her from their library. Where was Master Pole? He had taken himself off? But no matter. Peg must join them and help make way with the fresh-baked cakes and scones that he was missing.

There was no refusing their cheerful insistence.

Mistress Maude, buxom and rustling in bottle-green silk, starched cambric headdress, filled a pewter plate for Peg as Master Caxton poured a goblet of mead. He was wearing a linen bandage around his head. It had swathed his temples for a month or more, ever since the night that the Garden Tower had lost its giant elm.

Peg, waiting for his return on that stormy freakish night, and daring to hope that Young Edward and Dickon would be with him, had seen him stumble home alone through a sluicing downpour, soaked and chilled and dazed by a blow from a toppled brick.

"A one chance held out and lost to me. Lost to me!"

He mourned it over and over as Mistress Maude helped him to his bed, and Peg hovered with basin and cloths and salve to bathe a bleeding cut over his right eye and to sooth the knobby discolored swelling that protruded from his forehead.

"Lost, you hear me, my good Maude? Lost, Mistress Margaret. And the very handiwork of Satan himself, that searing crackling streak of lightning. A jagged flash—and there lay the severed boughs, and there lay I, struck down as prone on the ground as they. And all around me bricks and rubble and then people crowding and exclaiming—thunder clapping overhead—— Bedlam! And what for it, what for it, when I could think straight, but to pick myself up and walk away? What other choice left me? None. None."

Master Caxton had thrashed in his bed through all the hours that remained of the night.

The next morning when he could bring himself to speak quietly and with some measure of resignation for his futile efforts, he told Mistress Maude and Peg that with the elm's crash and the toppling of the wall, the Inner Yard had at once been a-swarm with yeomen. Running from their rain shelters, they had gawked at the split trunk, the blasted boughs and the pile of mortar and brick, and then they had set a sentry to guard the little green plot until the gap in its wall could be repaired.

Without so much as a word said to him beyond excited comment upon the storm's havoc and the offer of an arm or two to steady him, Master Caxton had been allowed to walk away across the Tower Yard and through the Outer Gate.

An old bespectacled fat priest was what the Yeomen of the Guard had taken him for, nothing more. And right in part they were, for he had bulged like a meal sack with the coiled rope, that Young Edward had so joyfully guessed would be tossed him, hidden under his brown robe. More than that, there had been the two cassocks, two hoods, two books of psalters, that he had borrowed from the Abbey's choir stalls, strapped around his middle.

One chance. And never a hope for another.

By the end of August London was mulling as murky a bit of tavern talk as had ever come its way. A Tower jailer, his tongue loosened by too much ale, had babbled in a wharfside pothouse that the Upper Chamber of the Garden Tower stood empty. Overnight the Young Uns had left it tennantless. Done a skip, they had—in a kind of a way.

The gossip, leaking through Chepe to Westminster, reached the sign of the Red Pale in due course. And Peg, clutching Neddie the closer for it, never let him out of her sight.

One day, sitting under the trees in Master Caxton's garden, her sewing on her lap, she began to ponder upon Young Edward's thrush. What had become of it? In whose care might it be now, she asked herself. Who fed it these days? Who cleaned its cage? And was it lonesome? Might it have lost its song again, moping for sound of a familiar voice to chirrup to it?

She discussed the matter with Susan Dow, who, sitting next to her on the bench, had fallen into the habit of popping in at Master Caxton's at such hours as a brown-crusted meat pasty or a succulent tart could be expected to come out of the scullery oven.

Running her tongue around her lips to lick off gooseberry juice and snuffling, with a wet drop hanging ready to fall as usual from the end of her nose, Susan Dow offered the suggestion that she herself trip off to the Tower and make personal inquiry concerning the thrush.

"How else go about finding Master Chirp?" she demanded practically. "And who'd know better where he be than Lobster Legs, the sentry at the Garden House? You call him to mind—that silly fellow that I cozened once before? As to finding myself in hot water by making another visit, there ben't a chance. Who would harm old Susan Dow seeking out her birdie? Leave it to me, duckie. I'll speak out mealy-mouthed as ever was heard when I reach the Tower Gates. And down on my marrow bones, I'll go to every yeoman in the Yard if need be. You'll see! I'll have your thrush back quick as any wink."

Away she went without delay, despite Peg's anxious de-mur. But her long trudge through lanes and streets and al-leyways was all for nothing. Once she had wheedled and whined and bandied her way into the Tower Yard and past the Middle Gate, there was little information to be gained from the scarlet-hosed sentry who stood guard at the Garden House portcullis.

"Turned up again, have you, Mother Drip-Nose? And what brings you back?" he wanted to know. "Be it a skewer-ing through your ribs that you're asking for?" He lowered his sharp pointed halberd with a pretence at a thrust, and snickered when Susan Dow leaped aside, squawking indig-nantly. "What's the trouble, Granny Snivels? You be hop-ping around like a chicken on a hot paving. And out with it. Out with it. What be your business here, this second time?"

" 'Tis no more than the fetching of the Young Un's song-ster home with me, Lobster Legs, and why not come after it, seeing as I have a fancy for the birdie now that His Highness ben't about to look after it? Will you hunt it up for me, pretty boy? There's a good lad——"

"A bit on the slow side with your asking, old woman. To find the thrush at this late day I'd need to search till the cows come home."

"The birdie be gone from here?"

"Right, gammer. 'Twas set free in the garden yonder when His Highness—took leave, let's put it—of the Upper Chamber. But where it flew, once out of its cage, how would I know?"

"Flew—a warbler with a broken wing? Not likely, Lobster Legs."

"Say hopped then, if it suits you. But no place for argument, a sentry box, old woman. So off with you now. On your way. On your way. And blow your nose, mother! If 'tis a kerchief you lack, why not use your skirt hem?"

With the sentry's guffaw following her, Susan Dow turned her back on the Garden House and flounced off to admit defeat when she reached the Red Pale.

Peg, with the thrush forever out of reach, concerned herself over it more than ever. Had it perished of hunger and thirst, crippled as it was, and inept at finding sustenance for itself? Or had it perchance been a victim of the first hawk that swooped over the little green garden? And what of its shivering plight when winter came, bitter and wet?

It was Master Caxton who gave comforting answer to her

questions with query of his own. Was it not entirely possible, entirely natural, that the thrush had discovered almost
at once how to peck for bugs and seeds and worms? As to its
thirst, would there not be a fountain in the garden or a ditch
of one kind or another? And could the smallest of bushes
not provide sufficient shelter for the thrush, or even a nesting place should it chance to find a mate? Most certainly.
And a delight, truly, to contemplate the song that would be
pouring more joyous, more sweet than ever from its white
throat now that a cage and captivity were things of the
past.

But there was yet greater comfort than that to be had from
knowledge of the bird's abode in the garden.

"Would your sadness not lighten, child, if you thought
on Young Edward and little Dickon lying somewhere close
to the thrush, somewhere in sound of its trilling?" Master
Caxton had asked Peg gently. "Then, why not accept it
as so? For where else their grave but in the Tower confines,
if they be murdered as we must steel ourselves to believe?
Would Gloucester's hireling, whoever they were, have
dragged them further? Nay. Too great a danger, too great a
haste dogging their heels. Your cousins sleep near, or in,
the Garden House, I be certain. And a happy thought, you
agree, that the thrush sings to them and that they hear? For
my own part, I shall cherish the conviction whole-
heartedly. Blithe bird, blithe princelings. And ever a summer day for them."

Chapter Fourteen: ON THE MARCH

"Richmond is on the seas—
He makes for England, there to claim the crown."
Richard III, Act IV, scene 4.

What a great many things Master Caxton's linen bandage recalled to mind and how far astray one's thoughts could wander.

Peg, nibbling the cakes pressed upon her by Mistress Maude, reflected soberly on the events of the past month. All of them beyond remedy, alack. All of them best forgotten. And now, without further rumination or further dallying, she must fetch her sewing bag, sort a tangle of embroidery silks, put on her thimble and turn immediate attention to a bit of handiwork that cried out for completion by the morrow.

The next morning when Sir Golden Cap reined in his horse to say a last good-bye to Master Caxton's household, he was presented with two gifts. Both were wrapped in squares of brown cloth and tied with hemp string. Untying the knots of one, he found that Mistress Maude had sewn him a fine soft linen shirt to be worn under the chain-mail hauberk that would case him in time of battle.

Peg's package held a pair of leather gauntlets.

Pink as a rose, she watched him draw them on. They had cost her hours of cutting and firm stitching and a month of painstaking effort embroidering their flaring cuffs with a pattern of leaves and flowers and a scrolled tracery of gold-thread lettering.

" 'Spes in deo est,' " Master Pole had spelled out. " 'Hope is in God.' " His hazel eyes met Peg's gravely. "My thanks to you, Mistress Margaret. A gift I shall treasure, believe me."

He took the road to Wales then, and found it a long one. When would he retrace it? He wished he knew. Too brief, his stay in London. Would he ever see home again, that quiet shire of fertile vales, of wooded hills and clear streams where his parents' manor lay?

But a waste of time, dreams, to a youth such as himself. Forget London. Forget home. With the way of the world so evil, and with naught but uncertainty and talk of combat in the air, Milford Haven alone held reality.

Milford Haven. How weary he had grown of it! A tawdry town. A bleak and cheerless camp. Months and months of monotony behind him. Months more ahead. And when tents were struck at last, the waiting done and a field of combat decided upon, how find the courage to face its carnage?

Horribly fearfully different, a battle, than commonplace joust or tourney or archery match. His clean untried sword, his shining lance smeared with blood. His azure arrow, red-dyed over its blue.

And for himself, what? A pike thrust through a groin? A cleaved skull? Spear point between his eyes? A lopped-off hand or leg?

Qualms and misgivings as to his courage rode neck-and-neck with him and other doubts as well troubled Sir Golden Cap. A man, aye, even a coward doubtless could somehow stand fast, somehow gird his loins to do his duty if the cause he championed held true merit. But was Henry Tudor's banner worth the price? And when at last on some distant day of its unfurling, would it float over England any less sullied, less tarnished with dishonor than Crook-Back's standard? Who knew? Who could say?

The dusty road unwound. The miles dropped away. Wales drew closer. And with Milford Haven reached, Sir Golden Cap found that it offered no fresher news of the Earl of Richmond's landing and campaign plans than it had months earlier.

Again, the stale town with its taverns and its street wenches and its shoddy carnival stalls, all greedy to catch at a soldier's purse, all playing upon his loneliness. Again, camp, dreary and apathetic and grown slack with its waiting.

Night after night, Richard Pole bedded himself in his tent and stared out at the little meadow beyond. With the passing of autumn he saw the last of its flowers curl and blacken under frost. Heard the icy tinkle of its streams running through grass that was brown and brittle and hoar-rimmed.

Winter, then, with him shivering, wrapped in his cloak.

A wet February thaw after that. Another spring. Another summer. Winter once more.

Half a dozen times during the long slow-passing months, Sir Golden Cap found one way or another to send letters off to London. Half a dozen times Peg knew the rapture of breaking a wax seal. Once, taking up pen to answer him, she had news to tell concerning Henry Stafford, Duke of Buckingham. All for naught, now, his weather-vane change of politics, his last minute schemes to bask in the Tudor's favor. Richard of Gloucester had caught up with him. He had been beheaded in the market place of Salisbury Town on a rainy November Sunday. The murmur of the river Avon and the toll of cathedral bells ringing out on All Soul's Day requiem were the last sounds he heard upon earth.

A second long winter set in.

Mistress Maude gave Peg linen to hem for sheets of her own, gray goose down for the stuffing of quilts, wool to card and spin into blankets and an elm-wood chest for their storing that was padded with bags of anise and lavender and orris against danger of moths.

Briskly, she kept Peg to the steady task of filling it. "Speed your needle, child," she would urge. "And mind you keep your wheel turning. Must I remind you over and over that some fine day you will be wishing to spread a marriage-bed? And what then, should you be caught empty-handed when a husband appears in the offing?"

"More like I'll die a virgin, Mistress Caxton," Peg made

answer more than once, her cheeks burning. "For who would speak my hand, think you? No one. No one at all."

"You've set your mind stubbornly to it, have you? Ah well, we shall see, we shall see." Mistress Maude had smiled wisely. "For remember, child, let today lack what it may, there be always tomorrow."

And so Peg has spun and hemmed and waited.

Through all those cold endless days there was the thump and clank of Master Caxton's press overhead and the smell of ink and wood-cut dyes floating from the loft of the Red Pale.

Smudge-faced apprentices toiled at the type-setting bench, their sleeves caught up and gartered out of their way, grimy goatskin aprons tied round their middles.

Master binders stitched and laced.

Leather toolers etched with red-hot needles.

A monk from the Abbey, sucking his badger-hair brushes to a fine point, jeweled chapter headings and margins with glowing color. Amethystine purple, sapphire blue, the green of emerald and beryl, vermilion deep as rubies, and on every page, a wash of purest beaten gold-leaf.

Often when the day's work was done, Master Caxton would gather his household together to read aloud from the latest book that he had printed and bound for someone or other of his rich and distinguished patrons.

First, a rush light must be set on a three-legged table

close to his favorite high-backed chair and a bowl of cracked walnuts and almonds put at hand, as well as a small and precious blown glass goblet from Venice that brimmed with malmsey should his throat grow dry.

Next, his curling-toed pointed slippers must be warmed by the hearth blaze, their soft leather as brown as his long woolen hose, his wool tunic, his velvet doublet.

After that, there was the careful adjustment of a small brown velvet skull cap to ward draughts from his graying sparsely-locked head. And then, opening a big beautiful volume, with his wrinkled neck thrust forward like a turtle's as he strained and squinted through his spectacles, Master Caxton would hold even drowsy-eyed supper-stuffed Neddie awake with tale after tale of chivalry and high adventure.

As for Peg, sitting at her loom, her eyes big and bright, her lips parted as she listened, it was only when Master Caxton read of a brave young squire and of the king's daughter whose talisman he wore, that she longed to stop her ears, longed to shut out the sound of his voice.

With winter passed, spring burgeoned once more. And this year, along with its breath of bluebells and primrose and hawthorne, its burst of bud and flurry of new leaves, it brought the zest of expectation to both stay-at-home Londoners and to men in far places.

A magic stir ran through the camp at Milford Haven. Battle-harness and stirrup leathers were oiled. Cuirasse and steel basinets polished. The cutting edge of halberd and axe and billhook sharpened on grindstones that whirred all the day long.

And then upon a summer morning, a long-awaited fleet hove in sight, its sails billowed with a strong salt wind from France.

Richard Pole, standing on the cliffs above the harbor, watched it put in for shore and drop anchor. Scrambling down a gorse-covered hillside, he elbowed a way along the crowded wharf for a closer appraisal of the steel-bonneted knight who was being rowed ashore in a small boat. A slightly made and sallow-countenanced man, the Tudor, with a thin high-bridged nose, a narrow jaw, and a fall of straight lank brown hair to his shoulders. Narrow-eyed, too, he was, summing up the knights and squires and men-at-arms that swarmed quay and cliffs.

" 'Tis ermine or a shroud for him now, and well he knows it," Richard Pole told himself. "The die be cast once and for all to guess from the look upon his face."

It was with an upsurge of old doubts, old tremors, then, that Master Pole heard the blast of a silver trumpet and the roll of drums.

Henry Tudor, Earl of Richmond, had stepped ashore, a white satin banner blazoned with the Red Dragon of Wales waving over his high-held head. Kneeling, he kissed the soil and acclaimed it his, in the name of God and St. George.

The very next day, he and his seven thousand followers were on the march. Losing no time, and determined to strike rather than be struck, he was spurring his troops north and

east as swiftly as men and mounts and baggage wagons
could travel.

The acclaim of the countryside was in his ears like the
clamor of early-rung coronation bells.

"Up, a Red Rose! Up, a Tudor! Up, a Welshman!"

Every hamlet dweller, every moor and mountain man was
shouting it. For born of their own blood, was he not, this
Richmond, and bred from stock that went back to John
O'Gaunt, went back to the Cadwallader?

At Shrewsbury he crossed the Severn river, and Richard Pole counted a thousand more recruits who poured
into town to join him. Pushing on, the Tudor marched yet
deeper into England, and a week later had bedded his men
in the village of Atherstone and himself slept that night
at the inn of the Three Tuns.

His slumber was quiet; the ermine that he coveted all
but wrapped round him, and the shroud he risked put out
of mind.

A small folded sheet of parchment lay secure in a pouch
under his steel-mesh shirt. It had reached him by messenger while he ate his supper and drank his wine and drew
map after map with his spoon handle upon the white cloth
that was spread over the inn's plain plank table.

Two knights had put their signature to the parchment.
My lord William Stanley for one, his brother Thomas for
the other. With the pledge of their swords went the loyalty
of the eight thousand henchmen who wore their blue
shoulder-knots, their gold sleeve blazon.

Let Henry Tudor choose the field, they had written, and let him set the hour. Let him strike the first blow against Gloucester. Their turn, then, to flank the Boar on left and right and to close in gladly for the kill.

Call it a blow of avengement for the Princes in the Tower. Call it avengement for the death of the Earl of Rivers, and of Grey and Hastings and a host of other kinsmen and friends.

Last, but not least, call it a loyal blow for Richmond himself, the son of that long-suffering bereaved Lady Beaufort whom William Stanley, a widower, had espoused as his second wife.

Oh, a quiet sleep, assuredly, for the Tudor that night!

None of any nature for the Plantagenet. A few days earlier, with the scarce-to-be credited news brought him of Richmond's impudent march into the very heart of his kingdom, he had ridden out from Nottingham, his summer castle, a hastily-garnered army in his train, and galloped to Leicester, a town lying no more than several short miles from the Tudor's encampment.

Better far to meet an enemy face to face, sword drawn, than to be smote by surprise.

When his men were tented for a last night before they would bivouac upon whatever field might prove a battle ground, he took himself to an inn that boasted the ingratiating and newly-painted name of the White Boar.

His bowing hand-rubbing smirking host had set out a roast partridge for his supper and a boiled suet pudding that was served upon silver trenchers carried from Nottingham, and the oak-posted damask-canopied bed that awaited him was his own, hauled from his castle on a baggage wagon. With night closing in, he threw himself down on it, and having blown out his candle, lay in the dark, calling a silent roll over and over.

Woefully shrunk, his roster of fighting men. And how had it come about?

Only a week earlier, his black unwinking eyes had looked on easy certain triumph over Henry Tudor, the would-be usurper. Let him march on London, if he would, he and his rabble of Frenchmen and die-hard Lancastrians. What more to his attack than a small unweighty clash of arms? And with the Tower as bulwark against him, the Bridge a bristling span of bowmen and spearmen and artillerymen, and with Westminster Palace garrisoned to fortress strength, what end in sight but Richmond's head upon a pike? Richard the King had smiled coldly thinking on it. And then overnight the picture had changed.

Vaguely at first, as though blown on the faintest of breezes, a suspicion had crossed his mind that traitors and renegades were spawning like river salmon in every shire.

Here, a man turning coat. There, another.

The little chill breeze had begun to blow harder. Had become a wind. Had become a gale. Suspicion gave way to certainty.

He knew now that his assurance had played him false. His spies and informers had either been outwitted by his enemies, or had deliberately made him their dupe. No matter which, the kingdom that he had boasted as lying in the palm of his hand was split in two like an over-ripe melon.

Up, a Richmond!

Up, a Gloucester!

Nary an Englishman or a Welshman but was making the choice.

And a crafty sly fellow, admittedly, that exiled upstart from across the sea. Who would have looked for so early a landing of his Breton ships? Who would have thought his march to be routed north so surprisingly? Who would have believed that it could be so swift?

And of what vantage now, the Tower or the Bridge or the Royal Garrison, should the Tudor choose to do battle in the open countryside rather than to hurl himself against the walls of London?

The hour grew on to midnight and past.

The town of Leicester slept, except for a watchman going his rounds through the cobbled streets, and for Richard lying across his splendid bed, his black unwinking eyes fixed on darkness as he counted and calculated and made his tabulations.

Up, a Richmond! How many men cried it in all?

Up, a Gloucester! How many would fight and die to keep his pennant flying from its ashwood stave?

All well enough that my lords Catesby and Ratcliff and Lovel stood firm. Brakenbury and Norfolk. Surrey and Northumberland.

But what of certain others? Had his dangled prizes lacked sufficient glitter? Had his promises of land and castles and monies been deemed paltry?

How else explain the Stanleys' absence? Where were they, those two whose joint weight could tip the scales so heavily in his favor? Where were they, that shrewd and slippery pair, who for all their shilly-shallying would, at the last, play their cards with his, he could have sworn?

Over slow in mustering, the both of them.

Over slow.

To put trust in them upon the morrow or not?

There was the rub.

Chapter Fifteen: THE BOAR AND THE DRAGON

"Fight, gentlemen of England! Fight, bold yeomen!
Draw, archers, draw your arrows to the head!
Spur your proud horses hard and ride in blood.
Amaze the welkin with your broken staves."
                              Richard III, Act V, SCENE 3.

The rub, verily.

At the first seep of daylight through the shutters, Richard was a-stir and buckling on his armor. An hour later he had ridden out of Leicester at the head of his troops, with White Surrey, an arched-necked battle-charger, under him.

Foot soldiers marching four abreast on the dusty highway, baggage carts and cannon wagons lumbering and creaking through the ruts, cavalry horses prancing, his cavalcade advanced to the small neighboring market town of Bosworth. A halt there, that men and mounts might water at its well, and then on to a wide fallow field that stretched beyond the village outskirts.

No coward, Crook-Back. As boldly as the Duke of Richmond, though belatedly, he too had chosen to strike rather than be struck.

A little rise diapered with daisies and lush with clover

broke the field's flatness. Riding to its crest, Richard looked across the meadow to the far side where a glitter of sun-tipped lance and spearhead, a flaunt of rippling banners marked Henry Tudor's camp two miles distant.

A single glance and he knew past all uncertainty that his dangled prizes, his promises of castles and lands and monies had gained him nothing. The Stanleys had chosen to play a game of their own.

The two brothers had bivouacked on either side of Henry Tudor. The pennons of Sir William were flying mockingly a little to the right of Richmond's camp, and forward. The pennons of Sir Thomas fluttered to the left, and forward.

In the face of battle, Bosworth Field had assumed the outline of a crescent moon. Clearly enough, Richard saw that his grassy hill had become its vunerable tip. Nothing for it now but to deploy his troops to the best advantage left him and to set them to the speedy digging of trenches and the throwing up of breastworks.

The summer sun blazed and wheeled upon a day of fever-ish readying on both sides of the field. At its close, all four armies that fringed the meadow were dark and silent and ringed round with a doubled sentry watch.

Master Pole, encamped under the Red Dragon of Wales, had wrapped himself in his cloak and with battle accouter-ment spread beside him, his mount tethered close, was stretched on the ground, gazing up at the sky.

Stars. Stars. Myriad upon myriad of them, pricking the darkness. Countless, they were, as leaves in a forest. Countless, perchance, as all those other soldiers, like himself, who from the beginning of time had doubtless gazed skyward upon the eve of battle.

Might this be his last sight of the twinkling jewels hanging there? An open question, for with the dawn of day, Henry Tudor's buglers and Richard Plantagenet's would sound a charge.

And of what mettle would he prove when that fearful crash of men and mounts and weapons came to pass? If he but knew! And if the morrow but marked his second or his dozenth battle—any, any at all, rather than his first——

Vain, however, and wont to turn his blood to water, these musings on what the dawn held for him. Wiser, and more heartening by far, to fix his thoughts upon the sky once more.

How vast that canopy of night. How brilliant those stars, studding its velvet. Orion's cluster. Neptune. Jupiter. And there was Venus, all lustrous and pulsing. Venus, the planet of Love, aye, but outshone this night by Mars—

For all his sober contemplations, for all the hard ground under him, the ache of legs cramped by long days in the stirrup, the crying-out of his stomach for more to fill it than the field ration of salt meat and bread that had served for supper, Master Pole slept at last, heavily.

The stars faded. The night sky lightened. It was a trumpet blast from Richard's camp splintering the quiet of a rose and gold dawn that brought him to his feet, dazed and stupid and knuckling his eyes.

No more than half awake, Master Pole stumbled to his horse and tightened the metal plates, the leather straps, the steel-meshed trappings of its war harness. The greaves on his own legs to be secured then. His hauberk to don. He snatched it up, pulled it over his head; his fingers as they fumbled with the neck slit were as cold as the shirt's dew-chilled woven-steel rings themselves.

Next, his sword. There were shouts and neighing, tumult of men and chargers all around him as he girded his waist. A curse upon the tremor of his hands! Would the tongue of sword-belt buckle never meet its hole? Steel basinet last, with leather thongs to knot hurriedly, clumsily, under his chin, and its viser to clamp down.

And now to mount.

Swinging his armor-weighted body into the saddle, Master Pole reined to a post alongside of Sir John Manning.

Up a Henry!

Up a Richard!

To the blare of trumpets, the tattoo of drums, Tudor and Plantagenet took the field, plumes streaming from their helmets, banners flying, the early sun striking a gleam from pike and lance, from polished shield and buckler.

Wave on wave of Richard's archers rushed down his grassy hill. Steel-capped, leather-breeched, leather-corseleted, two thousand bowmen poured on to the meadow, spraying arrows as they ran.

Henry loosed a like flood. On the west, his cannon blazed

Tudor and Plantagenet took the field.

and belched from a crude unwieldy cart. On the east, Richard's few guns rumbled and strained to disgorge a spate of aimless scattered balls. Then in black futile smoke and a sputtering-out of acrid sulphurous fuses, the random fire ceased on both sides. The victory, on that August day in the year of Our Lord 1485, would go to archers and bowmen, billmen and cavalry.

Master Pole, plunging across the meadow, his sword flashing, his bay gelding neck-and-neck with Sir John's froth-flecked black, saw Richard's horsemen lunge to their first and terrible charge. Off the rise they were coming, with Crook-Back himself in the lead. White Surrey, cased in steel plate and roweled mercilessly by long-shanked spurs, was bearing him down the hill at a heavy pounding gallop.

The King of England. And a Crook-Back truly, sitting his mount squat and humped, his short neck thickened by a steel gorgelet, his burnished armor giving off a shimmering aura of light, his pointed steel shoes thrust hard through stirrups. Visor open. Thin lips curled in their cold sneer. Black eyes glittering, implacable. And around his helmet, shining arrogantly, the narrow gold crown of the Anointed.

Crash of steel against steel then. The bloody hack and cleave of battle-axe. The thud of knotted club, of spiked mace. The slash of sword blade. The shiver and splinter of lance. And louder than the trumpeting of bugles, louder than shouts and oaths, the frenzied scream of ripped and gutted horses.

Sir John, galloping toward the wearer of that vaunted

golden circlet, went down in the first five minutes of the charge with the flash of a bright sword hewing his left hand from his reins and a billmen's hook pulling him out of the saddle. Dragged to the ground, lying there star-fished, he was trampled to pulp under the on-rush of iron-shod hooves.

"Jesu! Jesu! God in Heaven rest your soul, my lord——"

The cry burst urgently from Master Pole who swept forward in a tide of riders. Savagely, he spurred deeper into the fray. Fiercely, he swung his sword.

A slicing blow for Sir John. Another for Young Edward. Another for little Dickon, and now his maiden blade was dripping to the hilt.

With a shout of praise and encouragement, a knight, jostling next to him, charged ahead, his glittering pennoned lance at the thrust. It was the Earl of Oxford, a Star with Rays the blazon on his shield. And the noble he did for, as his lance found its mark, was John Howard, Duke of Norfolk, if the Silver Lion worked on his pierced and bloody hauberk spoke truth.

Crook-Back had lost his staunchest supporter. And toppling beside him, having ridden up to defend his sire, was the young Lord Surrey, thrust through-and-through.

The morning advanced. The sun rose higher. The field was a red welter under its glare, its crisscross of little meandering streams incarnadined and choked with the dead, their banks a gory slippery mire.

Henry's first-line troops were succored by a second with the Earl of Pembroke in command. For Richard, the field was stiffened when the Duke of Northumberland charged down the hill in the lead of fresh cavalry.

Robert Brakenbury, Lord Lieutenant of the Tower of London, was down now, and Master Pole's sword the ruddier for it. The Cat was down, and the Rat. The Dog, proving craven, had fled.

Richard, having fought inch by inch across the meadow, was roweling White Surrey through a swampy rivulet that lay between himself and Henry. Guided by the flutter of the Tudor's banner, he hacked and trampled a way through a knot of slashing thrusting mace-swinging Welshmen and closed in on Henry.

Half blinded by the sweat that poured from under his leather-padded steel helmet and by the glare of the mid-morning sun that blazed with dazzling brightness on Henry's breast-plate and casque, Richard raised his battle-axe in swift arc and brought it down, crashing.

Let Satan take the Usurper! Let the Imps of Hell seize upon him!

Henry, jerking hard at the reins of his neighing rearing charger, swerved aside. It was Sir William Brandon, his standard bearer, riding next to him, who caught the full impact of the blow. With his skull split from frontal to chin, he sagged forward, drenched in a gush of bright blood. The ashwood banner-stave fell from his mailed fist. The fluttering green and white sarcenet pennon was on the ground. In another instant White Surrey's plunging hooves had shredded it into a rag.

And then in that very moment of the Red Dragon's ignominy, and while Richard's blinded eyes strained for another truer blow, and while his arm swung back and up in a second arc, a trumpet blew, sounding a loud clear charge.

True to their promise, the Stanleys were taking the field. On right and on left, their fresh troops were reinforcing Henry's.

Up a Tudor! Up a Welshman!

Up a Lancastrian! Up a Red Rose!

The battle cries were all for Henry. There were none now for Richard Plantagenet. None for the Boar. None for the White Rose of York. Rout and confusion, dispersement and flight had split Crook-Back's ranks. With the surge of Stanley henchmen across the meadow, he was left to fight alone, his tip of crescent moon a shambles of dead and wounded.

Dizzy and reeling in his saddle from a thwacking blow that had dented his helmet, he was hemmed in ahead and in the rear and on both sides by a rush of exultant, jeering foes.

Another blind hack. Another vain try at parrying. A splitting, close-up blow striking home then, and his right shoulder cleaved through to the bone.

With his arm dangling uselessly, all the strength of his body running out in a warm crimson tide, the dazzling summer day darkening for him, he was being pushed back, back to the swampy rivulet that he had crossed earlier.

Its bank was quagmire. White Surrey, gashed and winded,

nostrils flaring, agonized eyes rolling, began to flounder. For all of Richard's vicious roweling, the horse mired to his hocks. Laboring mightily under the weight of his steel harness, he staggered, and sank belly-deep in mud.

Gallantly he was up again. But with the tearing sob of his hard-caught breath, his straining roll and heave, White Surrey lost his rider. Richard was unhorsed for all his fierce knee grip, his frantic clutch of reins.

The Tudor's henchmen let him stagger to his knees, and then to his feet. But when Master Pole saw him next, he was lying dead, face down in the swamp, slashed with the hack of a hundred swords. His crown had fallen off and rolled away under a hawthorn bush.

He was lifted up then and stripped of his burnished armor. Naked, he was tied to the back of a herald's mount, his head lolling on one side, his feet dangling on the other. And with a rag-tag, motley crowd of soldiers and gawkers from the village staring at him and spitting and throwing stones, he was carried back to Leicester for such potter's-field burial as the Gray Friars of St. Mary's Church might find goodness to grant him.

That same afternoon, as the long gory summer day waned, the Duke of Richmond stood before his assembled army and was crowned with the gold crown that had so lately rolled in mire.

Lord William Stanley set it upon his head. A *Te Deum* was sung. The Tudor was King. And before he sought his royal tent to hold conclave with the nobles who would be his

Councilors, he laid the flat of his sword blade to the shoulders of a score of young squires who had acquitted themselves with especial honor and valor upon the field that had won him his throne.

Among them, receiving the accolade of knighthood, was Master Pole, a weary blood-smeared boy who was sick of battle and who only wanted to go home.

Chapter Sixteen: A KNIGHT AND HIS LADY

"The weary sun hath made a golden set.
And by the bright track of his fiery car,
Gives token of a goodly day tomorrow."
Richard III, Act V, scene 3.

"So, Sir Knight, you have wish to say farewell to soldiering?"

Henry Tudor put the question to Richard Pole between mouthfuls of the supper that had been laid for him in the taproom of the Three Tuns. He was quaffing a fine full-bodied malmsey from a silver goblet and, in the mincing French manner rather than the more forthright English, was making use of dagger point instead of fingers to help himself to meat.

Bosworth's blood-dewed field had dried. Its carmined streams were running clear again. The bodies that had strewn it lay buried under its trampled daisies. And although no more than a week had passed since battle, Henry, with complete and final victory in his grasp, was listening amenably to the pleas of his Welsh and English volunteers that they be honorably discharged from his army and allowed to return without delay to the various shires from which they had gathered.

In due course, Richard Pole's turn had come to step forward and make petition of his sovereign.

Henry was eyeing him with more than ordinary interest. "You be firm in your determination to sever link with my army? A loss to me, truly, and I be loath to see you go. Need I tell you that I laid my sword upon your shoulder right gladly and with pride, knowing that your bravery had been of special mark for a youth so few in years, so new to battle? And why not think twice before you bid adieu to arms? Your decision could be swayed, perchance? What say to a promise of advancement, a reaping of favors, should you remain in my service?"

"You speak most generously, Sire, but my answer is nay."

"And a final one, I take it from the thrust of your chin. But why so stubborn a refusal? You be no true warrior at heart, no dyed-in-wool trooper despite your prowess?"

"Far from it, Sire. Quieter pursuits call me. By your leave, I shall make for London at once and forget that ever I swung a sword."

"You be as outspoken as valorous, I take it, Sir Knight. But why this craving for London? Methought from what I've garnered that you be country-bred."

"And so I be, Sire. 'Tis only that——"

"Say no more. Say no more. A matter transparent as crystal to a knowing eye."

Henry Tudor stabbed a chicken giblet from the wooden trencher in front of him and munched consideringly. "I find that your English cookery lacks the savor of Brittany's," he

observed, "and its flatness due, I judge, to a regretful omis-
sion of herbs and scallions and wine from its sauces. I shall
see that they be introduced. But, back to this London sally
of yours. There be a wench or two or three in the offing?
You'll play the gallant? You'll cozen and kiss among them
to make sufficient amend for time wasted these past months
in camp?"

Sir Golden Cap colored. "Rather, I go to seek a wife,
Sire," he answered simply.

"Your pardon. I stand rebuked." Gravely, Henry Tudor
lifted his goblet to Sir Golden Cap. "I wish you success in
your wooing. You'll grant me the same, I trust? 'Twould
seem the pangs of love have pierced us both, albeit in my
case, the object of my hopes is but a phantom. Or so you
might well declare her, for she be unseen by me as yet. Unseen in flesh, that is. Known to my eyes by naught but a
painted ivory likeness. And known to my inward fancy by
no more than a flow of letters between us. A penning of
verse or two, now on my part, now on hers. An exchange of
scribbled philosophies—— But why go on? You have
guessed, doubtless, of whom I speak? You know my ambi-
tions concerning the winning of the Princess Beth for Royal
Consort? My ardent wish to heal old wounds by binding
the Houses of York and Lancaster close with such an alli-
ance? What say, Sir Knight, have you heard my desire
noised abroad? Spoken of freely, openly?"

"'Tis common talk, Sire, and has been for months on
end."

"And meets with the approval of my newly-gained subjects, I trust?"

For all the sardonic twist of his lips, there was something of eagerness in Henry Tudor's narrow sallow face as he waited for an answer.

"A most hearty approval, Sire, so long as the Princess be assured of kindness from Your Majesty, and of fair play when it comes to the restoration of the goods and lands that Gloucester wrested from her with his charges of attaintment and bastardy. For, mind you, she be looked upon with deep affection by Englishmen, Sire. Her Queen mother shares our esteem as well. And high time that a tide turns in their favor. They have suffered unduly of late in all manner of ways."

"Again, you prove yourself honest spoken. I own to a growing admiration for you, Sir Knight."

The King's bright deep-set eyes were reflective as he speared another giblet and pushed a bit of bread around his plate to sop its gravy. "An idea occurs. Tell me, you served as squire under Sir John Manning, if I be correctly informed?"

"True, Sire."

"And he was kinsman to the Queen?"

"By no more than distant cousinship, Your Majesty."

"And yet close enough in family tie to have put both himself and you on easy footing in the royal household, I take it? The Earl of Oxford, in bringing your name to my attention for the bestowal of your knighthood, told me that you passed a goodly number of your page and squiring days at Ludlow Castle?"

"As I did, Your Majesty. Young Edward and the Princess Beth termed me friend. We were children together, with playtime and lessons shared."

"And thus you be the very man I seek. Who better an emissary to my ladylove?"

Henry Tudor clattered his dagger to his plate, wiped his fingers on a damask napkin and pulled a silk purse from his doublet. Drawing out a small box that was fashioned of richly gilded Florentine leather, he pressed a spring. The lid flew open and Richard Pole saw a ruby and pearl en-crusted brooch.

"What say to a fair exchange of favors between us, Sir Knight? If immediate severance from my ranks were to be granted you, along with a speeding of your departure for London, would you carry this bauble to the Princess Beth for me?"

"Most willingly, Sire!"

" 'Tis a bargain then." Henry Tudor tossed Sir Golden Cap the little box. "You may take your departure with the dawn, my eager and fellow lover. And when you give the Princess her jewel, give her my pledge as well that I too shall ride to London, and with despatch equal to your own, once affairs of state be set in order here. Tell her also, that my impatience to see her waxes warmer with ever passing day."

"I shall carry your message faithfully, Your Majesty."

"As well I know, Sir Knight. My every confidence reposes

in you. But by the bye, answer me this, will you, before you take your leave? Be the Princess Beth truly a maid so flaxen of hair, so bluebell eyed, so delicate skinned as her likeness shows? You swear she be no hag, no shrew, fobbed off upon me by those wily and anxious advisors both here and in Brittany who first put thought of courtship in my head? She be neither sour faced nor sour tongued? She be not pock-marked nor thickly shaped as to midriff or ankle? Can you blame me for a hope that Providence has been generous with her charms? And believe me, a doubled, nay a tripled fervor to my wooing, should she indeed prove a White Rose for beauty!"

"And that you'll find her, Sire. A blossom without blemish in appearance, and thornless when it comes to disposition, my word upon it."

"So? Then a weight from my mind. And I credit your every word. For were the Princess ugly as a spider, crabbed as a sour apple, such honesty as yours would blurt it willy-nilly, that be certain!"

Henry Tudor laughed shortly as he pushed aside his plate and stood up. "A pity that I must loose you. Would I had three score of councilors and courtiers round me half so direct with words. But if go you wish, go you may, and now to your departure. I shall send immediate word of it to camp and to the Captain of Troops. And then off with you, it shall be, to your fair lady and to mine. And I envy you, Sir Knight."

With an arm lightly across Richard Pole's shoulder,

Henry walked with him to the open door of the inn. "On your way as though winged, my young messenger. And should Eros deal but half so kindly with me as the God of War saw fit to do, I shall know myself to be the most fortunate of all men living."

As he spoke, the Tudor's eyes went beyond the door to the quiet downs where wooly sheep cropped and cattle grazed, to apple and to cherry orchards, to meadowland and to little rivers, to steeples and to towers and to rooftops that lifted in the distance against a blue cloudless sky.

"England—the fairest isle that ever were. And mine. All mine."

With his murmuring of the words, Henry's hands clenched as though they closed fast upon the treasure of the whole world. And then abruptly, he broke from his reverie, and his arm dropped away from Richard Pole's shoulder as he swung round to the little group of noblemen who had gathered at a supper board of their own at the far side of the taproom. "I bespeak your attention, my lords. Lend ear, if you will. Who among you can tell me aught of Gloucester's remaining nephew? Of what age be he, that sprig born of his brother Clarence and of the Lady Isabelle Neville?"

"If I mistake not, he be no more than a lad of seven, Your Highness."

It was a knight by name of Sir Thomas Grovesnor who put down his wine goblet to answer.

"But a Plantagenet, and of the Blood Royal for all his tender years, you'll agree, my lord?"

Again, for a moment or two, Henry Tudor was speaking half aloud. "A Plantagenet. The last of the lot, and over-precious then, in some eyes—— What's more, the grandson of that Warwick who once flaunted so bold a Yorkist banner. Ah well, 'out of sight, out of mind,' so I've heard."

He turned to Sir Thomas. "The thought of the boy is an annoyance to me. An irritant. There be a rasp to it like a harsh wool shirt. A sting as of nettles. And a grave and careless error methinks to leave him unconfined in these early days of my rule. Why chance a new division of loyalties, a further stirring-up of dissension, however small the risk? And you know my dearest hope, that the Kingdom be done once and for all with civil strife? Then, why not put the Young Plantagenet behind a wall somewhere or other and let him be forgot? Speak, Sir Thomas. You can lay prompt hands upon him? You have knowledge of his present whereabouts?"

"I have, Your Majesty. Master William Caxton, the illustrious printer of Westminster harbors him."

"The boy lacks kinsmen?"

"Nay, Your Majesty, but they be few in number and women of advancing years, for the most part, with none among them but his uncle, the dead Edward, having offered a roof when he and his sister were orphaned."

"His sister? There be a maid? However, little danger to me there, I fancy. Let her go her way. But seek out the boy with all speed. I shall brook no slightest delay. Nay. Not in days, mind you, nor yet in hours."

"You'll not argue the point with me, Your Majesty? You think it entirely wise, entirely sound that the child be put in Crown custody?" Sir Thomas was frowning a little, his brows knitting with concern as he asked his questions. "You'll not reconsider, Sire? You have no wish to give the matter further thought?"

"And, why should I, pray?"

"Have you forgot then, Your Highness, that even Gloucester himself stayed his hand and left the boy unmolested?"

"He stayed it purposely, you think? And for what reason did the Boar hold off, I wonder?"

"Shall I put it plain, Your Highness?"

" 'Twould oblige me exceedingly, Sir Thomas. This squeamish softness on Richard's part be of much interest to me."

"Name him a man of some wisdom, rather than of softness, Your Highness. Another murder added to his score might well have proved a one too many. The Kingdom, let me remind you, has gorged its fill of them. Shall I name his victims to refresh your memory, Sire? There was his brother, first. And then Gray and Rivers, Hastings and Buckingham, among others who stood in his path. After them, the two princes. And more lately, his own wife, some say, though be it true or not I have no proof to offer. But I tell you bluntly my lord, had Gloucester dared to strike again, all England would have cried 'enough' and clamored for his head upon a pike."

"And so you offer me a warning, be that your intent?"

Henry's face had darkened, and then he shrugged. "Let us not clash, Sir Thomas. Doubtless you speak with judgement. And set your mind at ease. I be no butcher, no slayer of children. Only put Clarence's son behind walls, and I shall let him live as long a life as be his natural span. I vow it. But bear in mind my admonition that there be no lag in shutting him away, and let his prison be strong. The Tower, no less."

Once more Henry Tudor's hungry possessive eyes sought the downs and the orchards, the meadows and streams, the steeples and towers and roof tops of his newly wrested kingdom.

Forgotten and unobserved, Sir Golden Cap slipped out of the taproom. The next morning he was riding toward London, and as he mulled over what he had heard, he quailed, for all the valor that Henry Tudor had commended.

How face Mistress Margaret, knowing what lay ahead for Neddie? And was it fitting duty of his to carry her the tidings, or should he leave it to others? More worrying than that, how soften her hurt once she heard? Poor maid—Neddie shut away from her would be Neddie dead to her mind, so fond she was of him, so melting-hearted toward him.

All of his eagerness to reach London fell away from him. The miles unreeled too swiftly, like thread from a dropped spool, and then at the end of his long journey when he reined in at the sign of the Red Pale, he saw with mingled relief for himself and a sorriness for Peg that a company of halberdiers had gathered on the curb outside of Master Caxton's dwelling. Halberdiers who wore the plum and silver blazon of Sir Thomas Grovesnor.

A few hours earlier start had brought my lord to London just that much sooner than his own arrival, and one question at least was answered. Mistress Margaret had been told the worst, and the wounding of her had been none of his, thanks be! And now to her, with all the solace that lay at his command.

Hurriedly dismounting, and tossing his reins to a hostler boy along with a penny, Sir Golden Cap knocked at Master Caxton's door and was let inside.

A glad flurry of greetings met him as he stepped into the Hall. All the household had gathered there, he saw at once, bent upon wishing God-speed to a small boy who was going away.

Mistress Maude's motherly arms opened wide to him, and he was hugged close to her plump bosom. Master Caxton offered the warmest of hand clasps. Neddie, cloaked and capped, ran to him with a shout of glee and swarmed over him delightedly. Peg, putting out both small hands to him with a little cry of joy, was warm-cheeked with a quick betraying blush.

There was yet another person in the Hall, Sir Thomas Grovesnor himself. Standing a little apart, silent and sober faced, he exchanged a glance with Richard Pole that gave away his ardent wish that he might have been a hundred miles remote.

Peg had been packing for Neddie. Even now, with the brief momentary rapture gone from her face, she was stuffing a last toy into the leather traveling-sack that had once gone to Ludlow Castle and back, and that held Neddie's change of shirts and small breeches, tunics and stockings and night clothes.

"There you be!" She gave the strings of the sack a twist and a knotting. "And I trust that all is tidy for you, and that you'll find no buttons lacking, no holes in need of darning. Was ever shorter notice given of a visit to be paid? But now, with all in readiness, a last word to you, little brother. Will you promise me to be a good boy for Sir Thomas when —when off you go?" Peg bit her lips to steady them. "You'll not forget that one's conduct must ever be most circumspect, on paying a visit?"

"I shall be good as gold, sister." Neddie vowed it solemnly and then with a glance round him he stood on tiptoe to whisper urgent questions that were for Peg's ears alone. "Can you not persuade Sir Thomas to let you join me? And why did he not invite the both of us to the Tower instead of me, alone? 'Tis unfair that you be left behind. Have thought of what you will miss? Soldiers marching round and round the walls every day, as Master Caxton declares they do. Drum and fife music. Bagpipes playing. Yes, and guns going off, for there be cannon in the Tower Yard, did you know it, Peg? So much to hear. So much to see. Do come!"

There was the faintest shadow of misgiving dimming

Neddie's anticipation as he tugged at Peg's hand. "Say you will. I shall miss you. I shall miss you very much, Peg."

"Foolish little Neddie! I never heard the like. Miss me, indeed. Be you in swaddling clothes then, that I must tag you as would a nurse? And do big boys such as you have need for their sisters' constant company?"

"Nay, mayhap not, but be you quite certain that I shall find some one at the Tower for playfellow?"

Neddie asked it plaintively, as he had asked a question like it on a day when he was astride a pillioned palfrey that was plodding through Shropshire mud.

"You shall have a dozen if you like. Have you forgot that Sir Thomas promised you games on end of quoits and darts and ball-tossing with the children of yeomen and warders? And have you forgot, too, that Susan Dow will lodge in your chambers to make your fire and cook your meals and to turn down your coverlets when night falls? Was it not good of her to give up service at the Palace that she might wait upon you? Was it not good of Sir Thomas to allow Mistress Maude the making of so pleasing an arrangement?"

"Susan Dow! An old hen!"

"Now, now, Neddie, no thrusting out of your tongue if you please. Susan Dow is most kind, and she be fond of you, truly fond. She—she has ever had a warm place in her heart for boys."

"But what if I should chance to grow weary of the Tower? May I come home, whenever I choose, Peg? Will you fetch me back the very moment I send you word?"

Peg bent hastily to straighten Neddie's stockings. "Shall we speak of that another day, little brother?" she managed to answer. "Shall we leave it until——"

It was Sir Thomas who stepped forward and filled the silence left by her trailing words. "We must go along, you and I," he told Neddie. "The afternoon be all but done. Our row downstream will be by pitch flare lest we hurry along."

Obediently, contentedly, Neddie took the hand he held out. The two of them made their farewells all around, and Neddie wriggled away from Peg's last hard hug. Then they walked out of the door, a servant following with the leather traveling sack. The halberdiers formed a little square around them. Turning toward the river, they took their way to a watersteps and to a waiting barge.

Peg, clutching fast to a little wooden whistle that Neddie had dropped, watched until they were beyond sight, and then she ran out of the hall, past Mistress Maude and Master Caxton, past Sir Golden Cap, to take refuge in the garden and to crouch on the bench under the beeches, sobbing as though she would never stop.

Mistress Maude, troubled and compassionate, bade Sir Golden Cap follow her. "She be distraught, bleeding-hearted, our Margaret, and has been since noon when Sir Thomas came to us with warrant for Neddie's custody. So offer your comfort now, dear lad. Let her lean upon it. And my only wish that it give her strength."

In the garden, Sir Golden Cap knelt under the beeches and put a hand on Peg's sleeve. " 'Tis I, Richard Pole. Will you not look up at me? Will you not stay your tears? Please. And if I fetch your hood, will you walk with me along the river before darkness falls?"

Without waiting for an answer, he went back to the house for Peg's mantle and then led her out of the garden. Passive and dulled with grief, she stumbled along beside him, her eyes swollen and unseeing, her gray bodice stained with the fall of her tears.

The path that Sir Golden Cap chose, pursued its way along a well remembered bank that was starred again with the purple asters, the white and yellow daisies of late summer. Picking a little bunch he folded Peg's fingers over it.

When they had come to a green awning of willows, he spread his cloak and drew her down on it. The white swans of another year were floating past, ducks and wild geese traced a familiar pattern against the sky, and Sir Golden Cap took up his idle pebble-tossing as though he had left off only yesterday.

In silence, and with listless disinterest, Peg stared at the widening ripples that lapped at rushes and lily pads. Once, she turned her white face, pinched and bleak with misery, to strain tear-blurred eyes for a glimpse of the Tower far downstream.

"Be glad that it lies beyond sight, mistress." Sir Golden Cap put a hand over one of Peg's, lying limp in her lap, the daisies and asters fallen out of it. "What be the use, searching it out? Why stab yourself so cruelly?"

Ignoring her unhappy silence, her unheeding ears, he began to talk to her, upon any subject at all that came to mind. His soldiering. The camp at Milford Haven. Bosworth Field. The sword's stroke that had bestowed knighthood upon him. The manor house and the quiet vales and meadows and woodlands that waited him now that he was free to go home.

And then he told her about Henry Tudor and the pearl and ruby brooch that had been entrusted to him. He would deliver it to the Princess Beth on the morrow.

Peg, lost in a bitter world of her own, heard him out indifferently and with little grasp of his words, or so it seemed, but when he had come to a close, being unable to think of anything further to relate, she ventured a question so low-voiced that Sir Golden Cap could scarcely catch it.

"You serve willingly as messenger between those two? You'll suffer no pang, no repining, should my cousin become consort to the Tudor? You have no wish that Beth might bestow her hand elsewhere, had a Princess Royal choice in such a matter?"

"None, Mistress Margaret. And why should I, in your opinion?"

Peg, eyes cast down, plucked at the daisies in her lap. "A comely maid, my cousin," she murmured. "Most fair, her countenance."

"Aye. Pleasing enough, true," Sir Golden Cap agreed as he tossed another pebble whose ripple caused a white water lily to tip and right itself on the river's quiet bosom. "Not that the King's taste be mine. Each man to his own, I say."

Peg lapsed into silence again. Once more her desolate eyes sought out an impossible glimpse of the Tower. Once more, they brimmed and blurred.

Sorry and at a loss for words, Sir Golden Cap sat beside her pondering a long moment. What to say? What to do, for the comforting of Mistress Margaret's heartache?

On sudden impulse, he reached to his wide belt and pulled out the pair of gauntlets that were thrust there next to his white tunic. The gauntlets that Peg had sewn for him. The palms were worn and soiled now, dark with his own sweat, dark with the sweat of his mount and the froth of champed bit. Dark with rusty stains that he had no wish to name.

Taking Peg's hand, he forced her reluctant fingers to trace the gold threads that twined their lettering on the cuffs.

" '*Spes in deo est.*' A heartening ring to the axiom, mistress, as well you knew when stitching it. Speak it aloud. 'Twould ease your gloom, methinks, to ponder its meaning."

"Nay, I'll not!" Rebellious all at once, Peg tried to free her fingers as she lashed out despairingly at Sir Golden Cap. "The words be hollow. A mockery. Who but a fool would mouth them? Who but a fool would find truth in them? 'Hope' you prate, for such as I? I, who stand alone, now that my Neddie be gone from me? I, who have no one in all the world? I, who—who have nothing—nothing? Oh, let me be. Let me be! Take your preaching elsewhere. Would I were dead. Dead——"

For all his pitying gentleness, Sir Golden Cap's hold stayed firm on Peg's struggling hands. "Speak the axiom as I bade you, mistress. 'Twill serve as a purge to wash away your hurt."

"Nay! Nay, I say!"

Sir Golden Cap's hand tightened. "Put tongue to it, mistress," he commanded quietly.

Because there was no denying him, because his hard hold was bruising her wrist, Peg made a reluctant, faltering start. " '*Spes—spes in——*' Oh, unhand me, I beg you. Let me go! I hate you. Hate you! What concern of yours such words as I be willing to speak, or those I choke upon?"

"On with it, mistress. Finish. You heard me ask it of you, did you not?"

Peg brought it all out then, as though it had been dragged from her. " '*Spes—spes—spes in deo est.*' Now be you content? Then go away. Go away! Leave me."

"Must I, Mistress Margaret?"

Sir Golden Cap lifted Peg's hand to his lips and kissed the red bruise he had made. "You'll not let me stay? For was I not right? You heard for yourself the solace in those words you spoke? And now, I pray you to speak others as well. Try. Do, mistress. After me, now—say them, will you? 'No longer do I stand alone. From this day on I walk with my own true love, come what may.' "

" 'My own true love?' " Peg repeated it blankly. " 'No longer do I walk alone?' " Her eyes widened unbelievingly. "You mean? You mean—?" And then with Sir Golden Cap's arms around her, she was huddling close to him, clinging fast and weeping wildly.

The willows cast a long shadow. The late afternoon drew to its close. A tranquil dusk fell. Little by little, Peg's sobbing ceased.

Sir Golden Cap smoothed back the rumpled russet curls that had fallen from under her hood and, searching for a kerchief in her cloak pocket, mopped her wet cheeks and dried her swollen eyes.

She stirred in his arms at last. "Tell me more of your home," she whispered. "What of your manor house? Be there a garden adjoining?"

"Aye, love."

"Lavender grows in it? Thyme? Pinks?"

"Aye."

"And be there a dovecote close? Tilled fields? A lambing fold? A cattle byre? And your lady mother, your sire; they will welcome me?"

"As their own daughter."

Peg's questions spent themselves in a long tremulous sigh. "A sound of Heaven to it all, truly!"

Having no words, Sir Golden Cap held her closer, his heart full to bursting.

Sweet, sweet Mistress Margaret. Unhappiness had caged her over long. Pray God, she would fly free one day soon. And pray God his hapless thrush on finding a green and quiet nest would sing again.

AUTHOR'S NOTE

The Song of a Thrush is no more than a story of what might have been, for history gives us few facts concerning the childhood and early youth of Margaret and Edward Plantagenet. Even the exact dates of their births are open to question. It is only the accounts of their deaths that we find recorded with grim accuracy.

"Neddie," Earl of Warwick, having languished in the Tower of London for the greater part of his boyhood, was beheaded on Tower Hill by order of the first Tudor king of England, Henry VII. Twenty-odd years of life lay behind him.

"Peg," marrying "Sir Golden Cap," gave birth to a son who on reaching manhood was known to the world as Reginald, Cardinal Pole. Later in life, as the widowed Countess of Salisbury, she became governess to her godchild Mary Tudor, daughter of Henry VIII and Catharine of Arragon. However, upon losing favor in the king's eyes, and being charged with treason against the crown, she too, as Neddie had been, was beheaded upon the Tower block.

The Church of Rome has beatified her as a martyr to her faith. The words carved upon her tomb were of her own choosing: *Spes in Deo est*—Hope is in God.

Katherine Wigmore Eyre